CHINESE CLASSICS

THE ROMANCE OF THE WESTERN CHAMBER

Wang Shifu
Retold by Teng Jianmin

CHINA INTERCONTINENTAL PRESS

图书在版编目（CIP）数据

西厢记故事：英文 / 滕建民改编；顾伟光，李尚杰，
(美) 亨利 (Henry, T.) 译. -- 北京：五洲传播出版社，2011.8
ISBN 978-7-5085-2163-3

Ⅰ. ①西… Ⅱ. ①滕… ②顾… ③李… ④亨… Ⅲ.①杂剧－剧本－
中国－元代－缩写－英文 Ⅳ. ①I237.1

中国版本图书馆CIP数据核字(2011)第152763号

改　　编：滕建民
英文翻译：顾伟光，李尚杰，(美) 亨利 (Henry, T.)

策划编辑：荆孝敏
责任编辑：郑　磊
设计总监：闫志杰
封面设计：叶　影
设计制作：蔡育朋

出版发行：五洲传播出版社
地　　址：北京市海淀区北三环中路31号生产力大楼B座7层
邮　　编：100088
网　　址：www.cicc.org.cn
电　　话：010-82005927，010-82007837
印　　刷：北京冶金大业印刷有限公司
开　　本：889×1194mm　1/32
印　　张：3.75
版　　次：2012年1月第1版　2012年1月第1次印刷
定　　价：68.00元

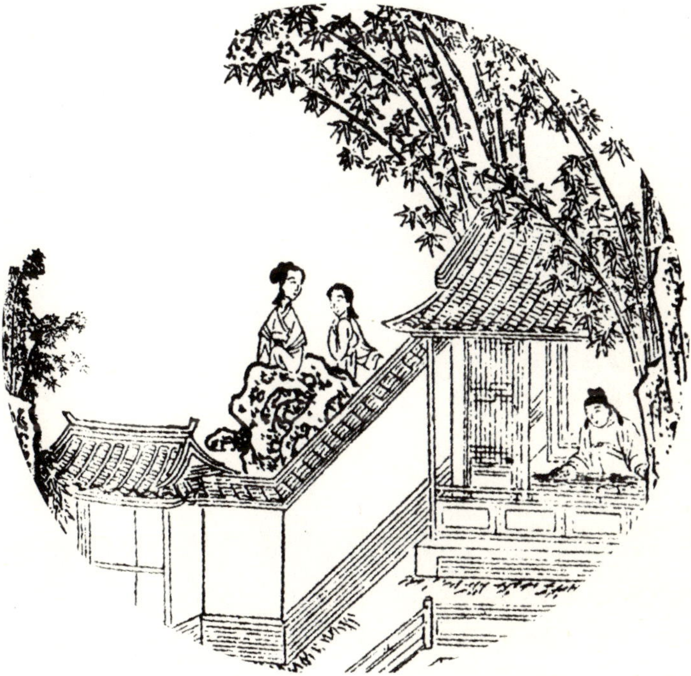

Contents

CHAPTER I 7
CHAPTER II 15
CHAPTER III 27
CHAPTER IV 37
CHAPTER V 47
CHAPTER VI 53
CHAPTER VII 65
CHAPTER VIII 75
CHAPTER IX 87
CHAPTER X 95

CHAPTER I

In the southwest of the Chinese province of Shanxi was an ancient city named Puzhou. It lay in Hezhong Prefecture, amongst the fertile middle reaches of the Yellow River, boasting majestic mountain ranges and lingering rivers. Rich in natural resources, the region produced a myriad of valuable products. As Hezhong borders the three provinces of Shanxi, Shaanxi, and Henan, it was a key thoroughfare for those traveling to and from the Tang Dynasty capital of Chang'an and the rich provinces of Shanxi and Hebei. What's more, Hezhong was the home of the Fengling Ferry, one of the most important ferries along the great Yellow River during the Tang Dynasty (AD 618-907). The prefecture thus attracted many government officials and wealthy businessmen, making it a prosperous and vibrant marketplace. The streets were constantly bustling with large crowds of merchants, hawkers, travelers, monks, soldiers and occasionally pickpockets.

Within Hezhong lay the Temple of Universal Salvation, a royal temple built for Wu Zetian – a Tang Dynasty empress, the only one in Chinese history, where she used to offer sacrifices and burn incense to Buddha, along with monks and pilgrims who came from far and wide to profess their piety. Incense burned all day and all night throughout the year, the smoke enveloping the magnificent temple in a halo of mystic beauty.

Later the temple fell down and the late Prime Minister Cui, acting under orders of the court, supervised its reconstruction. The abbot of the temple happened to be the monk who tonsured Cui. Despite the multitudinous crowds of worshippers that constantly thronged the temple, the monks nonetheless led a peaceful and serene life.

One day, two female pilgrims arrived along with an entourage of two servants. It was the late prime minister's wife,

Madam Cui and her only daughter, the 19-year-old Yingying. She was a fountain of talents, intelligent and capable, skilled at all that was expected of a well-bred lady: embroidery, poetry, calligraphy and much more. As was the custom of the time, her parents were responsible for arranging her marriage. When her father still lived, he betrothed her to Zheng Heng, the eldest son of the Imperial Secretary and nephew of Madam Cui. Everyone considered the marriage a perfect match. However, Prime Minister Cui passed away before the wedding ceremony could be held. As a devoted daughter, Yingying went into mourning for her departed father. During this time no preparations for the wedding could take place, and so the ceremony was delayed.

Among Madam Cui and Yingying's retinue was a clever and cunning maid named Hongniang. Having served Yingying since her childhood, their relationship was like that of sisters. Also in the group was young servant named Huanlang.

Abbot Faben found himself caught off guard by the visit of Madam Cui and Yingying, and he hastened out to the courtyard to greet them. Having not yet been informed of the prime minister's death, he was shocked to see the women dressed in mourning. He gradually learned of the death and that the grievers were escorting his coffin to the family burial ground in the town of Bolin, in Hebei province. However, the journey from Hezhong to Bolin was a long one, and there were only four of them. Wishing for a short rest, they entreated the abbot to accept the coffin into the temple and allow them to stay for a short while. While they waited, they sent a letter to Yingying's fiancé, requesting that he accompany them the rest of the way. The abbot immediately arranged for them to stay in a quiet compound of rooms called the Western Chamber.

It was then late spring. On one day, no pilgrims came to

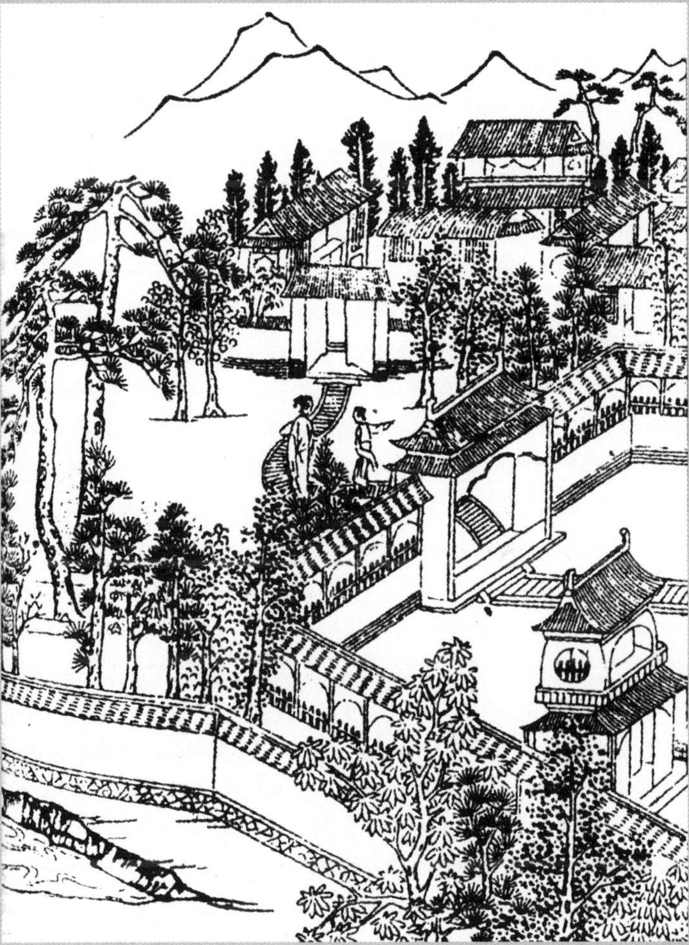

burn incense, and the temple sat in utter silence. As Madam Cui surveyed the solitary scene, she was filled with intense feelings of melancholy and loneliness. When her husband was alive they had resided in an extravagant home full of luxury: colorful silken clothes, choice foods, and hundreds of servants and guards. When she compared her previous life of opulence to her current state of bereavement, with only a handful of people to depend on, she could not help but feel forlorn and sick at heart.

As the only child, Yingying was the apple of her mother's eye. With her father gone, she became the only one that her mother could rely on. However, her own suffering over the death of her father and distress at the delay of the wedding caused her much unhappiness. Noting her daughter's state, Madam Cui became increasingly worried and anxious. Seeing how quiet it was that late spring day, she instructed Hongniang to take Yingying on a walk around the temple and cheer her up. While strolling through the temple's main hall, the two ladies encountered a young man.

His name was Zhang Gong but more commonly known as Zhang Sheng, meaning Scholar surnamed Zhang. He was a native of Luoyang. His father had been the Director of the Board of Rites, but both his parents had died of illness several years ago, and he was now on his way to the capital to take the imperial civil service examination. He had come to Hezhong to pay a visit to his old friend Du Que, with whom he had been as close to as a brother since childhood. But Du Que had decided to pursue a career in the military rather than in politics. Du took the first place in the imperial military examination and was now a general in command of an army of 100,000 soldiers charged with guarding the Puguan Pass. Because of the general's busy schedule, Zhang Sheng was unable to meet with him, so he came to downtown to find lodgings and have a look around. The innkeeper of the inn where he stayed told him of the city's famous royal temple with lacquered halls and Sarira pagodas, so he decided to go and see it for himself.

The monk Facong came out to greet him at the temple gates. Having offered him a seat and a cup of tea, Facong introduced himself as one of the abbot's disciples. The abbot had gone out and not yet returned, and he had asked Facong to receive visitors on his behalf in his absence and inform him of them upon his return.

"I came today to pay respect to the Buddha and visit the abbot. As he is not here, kindly show me around the temple, if you please" replied Zhang Sheng.

"With pleasure," remarked Facong. With these words he accompanied Zhang Sheng out of the room. Bringing all the temple keys with him, he opened the doors to the Prayer Hall, the Bell Tower, the Pagoda Garden, the Arhat Hall and other sacred places within the temple. Zhang Sheng could not help but marvel at the magnificence and exquisiteness of the buildings.

As they spoke, the pair walked along the winding corridors and into the Buddha Hall where they heard the soft voices of two young ladies. Zhang Sheng then saw Yingying and Hongniang emerge from the shade below the trees. It was quite clear that one was the maid and the other her lady, both as beautiful as goddesses descending from the heavens, particularly the lady. Despite her white mourning clothes and grief-stricken face, her elegance of movement and enchanting figure made for a beauty so charming that Zhang Sheng found himself at a loss. He had read about famous beauties before, but this was the first time he had beheld such heavenliness with his own eyes. Upon seeing the handsome young man entranced by her beauty, Yingying herself began to blush.

Zhang Sheng turned to Facong, "Are we not in a temple? How is it that I think I see a lady like a fairy that cannot be seen on earth?"

Facong smiled, "She is on earth. That is Miss Cui, daughter of the late prime minister." He then related to Zhang Sheng what had happened before and after the minister's death, adding that Madam and Miss Cui were both staying in the temple for a short while. This information caused Zhang Sheng to sigh longingly.

Seeing these strangers coming their way, Hongniang led her young mistress out of the Buddha Hall. Yingying turned around to give Zhang Sheng one last look before leaving. The young man stood as if in a trance, gazing at the breathtaking beauty as she slowly walked away.

After they left, Zhang Sheng turned to Facong and informed him that before long he would leave for the capital to take the imperial civil service examination. He planned to stay in Hezhong to make his final preparations for the test, but the inns in town were crowded and noisy, making them unsuitable for study. He then asked Facong to do him a favor and ask the abbot if he would rent Zhang Sheng a quiet room in the temple where he could review for the test. He added that his stay would not be long and he would pay well.

Facong passed his request on to the abbot who agreed, recognizing Zhang Sheng's sincerity, and arranged for him to stay in a room in the backyard.

CHAPTER II

Ever since her arrival at the temple, Madam Cui would spend her days burning incense and reciting Buddhist scriptures in the honor of her deceased husband. Wishing for the abbot to arrange for a Buddhist funeral ser vice, she sent Hongniang to meet with him and plan out the details.

Upon arriving at the abbot's room, she saw him conversing with a handsome and refined young scholar, discussing the renting of a room in the temple. After announcing her presence, Hongniang questioned the abbot about the possibilities for the funeral service.

The abbot said, "The fifteenth day of the second lunar month is a befitting day. Please tell Madam Cui that we are honored to perform the service and everything needed for it is already prepared."

Hongniang replied, "Excellent. Would you mind if I take a look at the Buddha Hall so that I may relate it to my mistress?"

The abbot stood up and said to Zhang Sheng, "Sir, kindly wait here a moment. I'll go show the hall to this young lady and be back shortly."

Zhang Sheng, having nothing to do, asked if he could go along with the pair, and the three of them set off for the Buddha Hall. Zhang Sheng politely allowed Hongniang to go first, and she made a note to herself of his good manners.

Once inside the hall, Hongniang asked many questions about the service's preparations, looking around to ensure that everything was properly laid out. Zhang Sheng wanted to strike up a conversation with the girl but she barely paid him any attention. Satisfied with the meticulous preparations, she expressed her gratitude to the abbot on behalf of Madam Cui. The abbot told her that everything would be ready, and Madam and Miss Cui need only come to offer some incense. Finally, he remarked how moved he was by Miss Cui's filial piety for her father, and that he would personally see to it that the service be ready before the end of her mourning period, so that she might repay her father's love and care on the anniversary of his death. As he spoke this, he suddenly noticed that Zhang Sheng was quietly crying. The abbot asked him what was wrong, and he replied, "A young woman such as Miss Cui has shown so much devotion to her parents. Myself, I've wandering around these years, away from home town and haven't even offered my parents one single piece of ritual money since their passing. I'm so ashamed! I hope you can have mercy on me and allow me to offer some incense and joss paper in honor of my parents. I believe Madam will not object, as she will understand my filial duties."

The abbot was sympathetic to his request and gave him permission to perform the memorial rites. The abbot then invited Hongniang to return with him to his room for a cup of tea, but she worried that Madam Cui might need her right now, so she thanked the abbot and was about to go back to her quarters. Once outside the hall, she ran into Zhang Sheng in the hallway, apparently waiting for her. He came forward and bowed.

"You must be Hongniang, Miss Yingying's maid."

Glancing at him, she forced a slight bow and replied, "Yes, I am. How may I help you, sir?"

"My name is Zhang Sheng. I am 23 years old and a native of Luoyang. I was born at midnight on the 17th day of the first lunar month. I'm not yet married…"

Hearing these words, Hongniang felt that the young man spoke too boldly, and she became annoyed.

"Who asked you about these things?"

Noticing her impatience, he approached a little closer. "Does Miss Cui often take walks outside of her chamber?"

This question really set Hongniang off. Her reply was dripping with irritation.

"You must've read many books, how is it that you don't know even the basic etiquette? What you said is beyond the pale! You must know Mencius' teaching that 'a safe distance should be kept between men and women'. As the old saying goes, a gentleman will neither adjust his shoe in a watermelon patch, nor his hat under a plum tree. Or as Confucius said, a man of letters should 'see no evil, hear no evil, speak no evil, and do no evil'. Madam is very strict with regards to Miss Cui's upbringing. The young lady is not so imprudent as to willfully show her face in public. If she sneaked out of her room, she would never hear the end of it from her mother. Regardless, Miss Cui has nothing to do with you, and you should take this to heart. You're lucky it's me telling you this and not Madam Cui, as she would not let you off so easily. She's very strict with others when it comes to etiquette, not to mention with her own daughter. From here on, you should know when to speak out and when to keep your mouth shut."

With that, Hongniang turned abruptly and went off to see her mistress. Her words had left Zhang Sheng speechless, and he slowly shuffled back to his room, sulking the whole way.

Hongniang returned to the Western Chamber and reported to Madam Cui on the arrangements for the memorial service, then went to see Yingying, to whom she repeated what she had just told Madam. While speaking about the service, she suddenly recalled the silly look on Zhang Sheng's face and burst out laughing.

Bewildered, Yingying asked, "What are you laughing at, you silly girl?"

Hongniang giggled and began to imitate Zhang Sheng's opening speech, bowing forward and stating, "My name is Zhang

Sheng. I am 23 years old and a native of Luoyang. I was born at midnight on the 17th day of the first lunar month. I'm not yet married…"

Even more confused, Yingying also laughed and asked, "What's wrong with you today? What's this nonsense?"

Hongniang then described the whole encounter to Yingying, including her scolding of Zhang Sheng.

"Sister, I really wonder what's going through this young scholar's mind. It's unbelievable that such a simpleton should really exist!"

Yingying thought back to the young man she had seen in the Buddha Hall the day before. He looked refined, not like some disreputable lecher. What's more, he had looked at her with obvious admiration. Yingying's heart began to beat a little faster as she recalled his bright eyes. She asked Hongniang if her mother had heard any of this.

"Not yet. If you wish it I'll go tell her straightaway," and she began to head for the door.

Yingying stopped her, saying "Let's keep this between us for now. You've already given him a sufficient reprimand, so we'll leave it at that. It's getting dark out. Please prepare the incense table; I'm going out to the garden shortly to burn some incense."

Hongniang placed the table in the garden and returned to accompany Yingying there through the side gate.

Shortly after his arrival, Zhong Gong had learned from a monk that every evening Yingying would go into the garden to burn some incense. That night he had gone to the garden early and hidden himself in a corner behind some rockery, hoping to catch a glimpse of the young beauty.

By that hour, most of those living in the temple were already asleep. The cloudless night was lit up by a clear moon and cooled

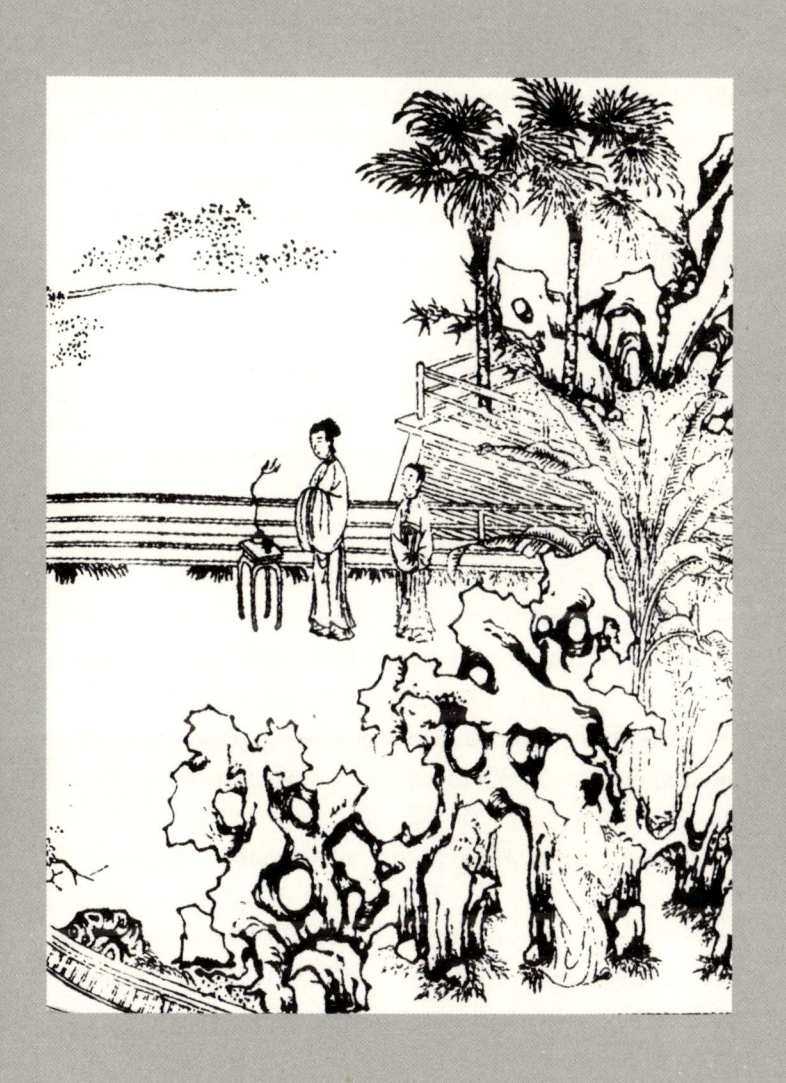

by a soft wind. The moon's light shone down on the garden, projecting shadows through the trees that seemed to be dancing with the wind. The leaves and branches appeared as if they had a silver lining, adding to the evening's mystique. As he admired the fragrance of the flowers and the beauty of the moonlight, he heard the side gate creak open. Shortly thereafter, he observed breathtaking figures of Yingying and Hongniang enter the garden.

Seen in the silvery moonlight, Yingying truly appeared as a moon goddess descending to earth. Her beauty and elegance froze Zhang Sheng in his place, and for a moment he forgot where he was and why he was there.

Yingying lit three sticks of incense and softly prayed.

"The first stick is for my father; may his soul swiftly ascend to heaven. The second stick is for my mother's continued health. The third stick is for…"

She paused. But Hongniang knew what she was thinking, so she broke in:

"Let me finish the third wish for you, sister. The third stick is for Miss Cui herself; may she find her Mr. Right as soon as possible."

Hongniang had taken Yingying's thoughts and turned them into words. The young mistress leaned onto the incense table and heaved a deep sigh.

Seeing all this, Zhang Sheng's admiration for Yingying only increased.

"I'm no poet," thought the young man. "I bet she has a good appreciation for fine poetry."

He began to recite a poem about her on the spot:

In the evening bathed in moonlight's shine,
When spring flowers cast shadows on the ground.

I look up and into the light of the moon,
Yet that beautiful creature is nowhere to be found.

Hongniang recognized his voice and remarked to Yingying, "This must be that 23 year-old unmarried loser."

Yingying had also overheard him chant the poem and knew it must be Zhang Sheng. Impressed by the originality of the poem, she answered with her own poem in the same form:

Solitude, her only companion in the chamber,
Witnesses the departure of springtime spent in vain.
He who cries out so,
Must share with the sighing maid her love!

Yingying's poem made Zhang Sheng's heart soar. He was now struck by not just her beauty, but also by her intelligence. How delightful it would be to sit beside her, composing poems together with such a lovely creature! With this thought still in his mind, he left his hiding place and approached the ladies, presenting himself with a deep bow to Yingying. She was about to respond when Hongniang stepped in:

"Someone is coming, sister. We should get back to the Chamber now, or risk Madam's displeasure."

With that, she dragged Yingying off. But before they were out of sight, Yingying turned around and cast a quick glance at Zhang Sheng. His heart leaped and he felt as light as if he could float. Back in his room, in the lonely light of his small lamp, he could neither study nor sleep; she was all he could think of.

On the fifteenth day of the second lunar month, the abbot and his disciples held the memorial service for the late Prime Minister Cui. As promised, the abbot let Zhang Sheng burn some incense for his parents in the Buddha Hall before the service began. Unsure if Madam Cui would disapprove if she found out, the abbot told Zhang Sheng that if she ever saw him and asked what he was doing, he should tell her that he is the abbot's relative and is burning incense for his parents. Zhang Sheng nodded his agreement.

Soon, drums and chanting of Buddhist scriptures filled the temple. The abbot invited Madam Cui and Miss Yingying into the Buddha Hall to offer incense.

The abbot told Madam Cui, "A relative of mine is staying here in the temple. He is a well-read young scholar. His parents passed away just a year ago, so he wanted to use this memorial service to offer incense and joss paper in memory of them. I agreed, but I fear you might be displeased with this intrusion."

"A relative of yours is a relative of mine," she replied. "Ask him to come over. I would like to meet him."

Zhang Sheng quickly came over to pay his respects to Madam Cui and once again he saw Yingying sitting next to her mother. They dared not speak to each other in her mother's presence. Nonetheless, Yingying used the opportunity to make a close observation of him. Recalling his splendid poem from that night in the garden, she could not help but be fond of this genteel and handsome young man. Throughout the service, Zhang Sheng also stole several looks at Yingying. He was completely captivated by her slim eyebrows, rosy cheeks and slender figure. He could never tire of looking at such beauty.

None of this escaped the attention of Hongniang who began to feel a little concerned, fearing Madam Cui might notice this exchange of admiring glances amongst the grand service. With the abbot and all the monks present, she also worried that they might come to their own conclusions if they noticed what was happening. As soon as the service ended she hurried up to Madam Cui. "It's getting late now and it's about time for Madam and

Mademoiselle to get back to the Western Chamber and take rest." She then accompanied Madam Cui and Yingying back to their living quarters. Following her departing figure with his

eyes, Zhang Sheng no longer felt like burning more incense and a sudden and overwhelming feeling of emptiness came over him…

CHAPTER III

It wasn't long before news spread that the late Prime Minister's wife and daughter were staying in the temple. Such news attracted the good and the bad, and among the latter was a group of bandits led by a man named Sun Feihu, nicknamed the Flying Tiger, with a troop of five thousand men that plundered and pillaged wherever they pleased. Hearing of the beauty of the young Miss Cui, he became intent on capturing her and making her his wife. With this in mind, he and his men surrounded the temple.

The monks were in a state of extreme agitation, having never been in such precarious circumstances before. Sun Feihu had his soldiers shout into the temple that if Yingying was not handed over within three days, they would set fire to the temple and kill everyone inside.

At a loss, the abbot informed Madame Cui of the demand, and the two of them hurried to Yingying's room to discuss their next move. Still reflecting on that day's meeting with Zhang Sheng, Yingying was beside herself and had scarcely eaten or drank anything all day. All she could think of was the sonorous voice and pleasing smile of that handsome young scholar. As she was silently repeating Zhang Sheng's poem in her mind, Hongniang interrupted by informing her that her mother and the abbot had come to see her.

Yingying bowed in greeting to the abbot. Not yet informed of the situation outside, she was a little surprised by the grim expression on his face and that of her mother.

"Have you not heard that Sun Feihu has the monastery besieged with his five thousand men?" her mother asked. "He wants to take you by force and make you mistress of his lair! My dear child, what shall we do?"

The news sent Yingying into a stupor. For days, she'd been

thinking about Zhang Sheng and their potential love, and had not paid the least attention to external events. Now, her mother's words made her feel as if the sky was crashing down and the earth rupturing open. She threw herself into her mother's arms.

"Now we have nowhere to go and nobody to depend on! What can I do?" she cried out.

Helpless, Madame Cui could do nothing but grieve in sorrow at their lamentable fate. Mother and daughter clung tightly to each other, tears flowing down their cheeks.

"As there is no other choice, you must hand me over to the bandits. I will sacrifice my body in order to save all the others," Yingying declared.

"I'm more than sixty now and death means nothing to me. But how can I lose my precious only child? You're so young and not yet married, how can I bear to see you fall into the hands of those terrible bandits, disgracing both your father and our family?" Madame Cui cried out.

The abbot intervened, "Let me go and ask the monks and laymen of the temple and see if they have any ideas on what we can do."

Yingying was resolute and declared, "Just hand me over to the bandits. This is the only way to guarantee the safety of my mother and those in the temple, as well as protect my father's coffin from desecration. There is no other way. However, I will never surrender my purity or disgrace my ancestors. Never! After I kill myself, you may hand my dead body over to the bandits. After I'm dead, it would be useless for them to harm you. If your life could be saved then my death will be worthwhile."

Hearing these heartbreaking words from her daughter, Madame Cui wailed in misery.

Yingying continued, "Since my mother cannot bear to be

separated from me, there is only one other way out. If anyone in the temple, monk or layman, can repel the bandits in any way, I will be presented as his wife and he will receive a handsome dowry. I would rather marry an unknown hero than a gangster like Sun Feihu."

Reluctantly, Madame Cui regarded it as a sensible plan. Thought it wouldn't be an ideally matched marriage, anyone would be better than Sun Feihu. She then asked the abbot to assemble everyone in the temple, and once they had gathered she declared that whoever could defeat the bandits would have her daughter as his wife.

Nobody said a word, until Zhang Sheng stepped forward and declared, "I know how to repel the bandits."

Yingying, seeing the bravery of the young scholar she had fallen in love, prayed that he could save her from the catastrophe. Madame Cui recognized this young man as the one who had offered incense to his parents, and asked him what solution he had in mind.

Before he replied, Zhang Sheng asked, "Madame, did you really mean what you have just said?"

"Yes, as I have already related to the abbot, whosoever can repel the bandits will have Yingying as his wife," she answered.

"Fine. As long as you mean it, I am going to tell you my plan on how to defeat the bandits."

Zhang Sheng first asked Hongniang to accompany Yingying back to her room before he discussed his plan with Madame Cui and the abbot. Madame Cui's impatience to hear all the details was evident.

Zhang Sheng began, "First of all, my plan will require the abbot's help."

"I'm no warrior. Better find someone else to help you with

THE ROMANCE OF THE WESTERN CHAMBER

this plan," the abbot said.

Zhang Sheng smiled, "Don't be afraid. I don't need you to fight them head-on. I want you to act as negotiator. Tell them that Miss Cui is now in mourning for her deceased father, and if her present state is disrupted then she must start again and all their efforts will be in vain. If Sun Feihu wants to marry the daughter of the Cui family, he must withdraw his army to the distance of an arrow shot. When the mourning period is concluded in three days time, the young lady will remove the mourning dress, don her bridal robe, and marry him."

"And after these three days? Will she really become his wife?"

"Don't worry. I'll get around and have everything under Control.".

The abbot went out of the temple and demanded an audience with Sun Feihu. Already impatient and irritated, the bandit leader rode over to the abbot in rage.

"Surrender Yingying now or I'll kill you and everyone else in the temple!" he boomed.

The abbot answered, "Calm down, General. Upon the order of the Madame Cui, I must give you some information." He then repeated what Zhang Sheng had told him.

Sun Feihu thought over the proposition. The abbot's words seemed to make sense; perhaps acting reasonably was the best course of action. Regardless, there was no way that Yingying could escape.

"Deal! Since the Madame has made this request, I'll give you three days. But if I don't get Yingying then, no one in the temple will survive! Tell the old lady she better live up to her word, or you'll all suffer the consequences! And let her know that it's very difficult to find a well-mannered son-in-law such as myself. She'd better consent to this marriage as soon as possible," the bandit

difficult to find a well-mannered son-in-law such as myself.

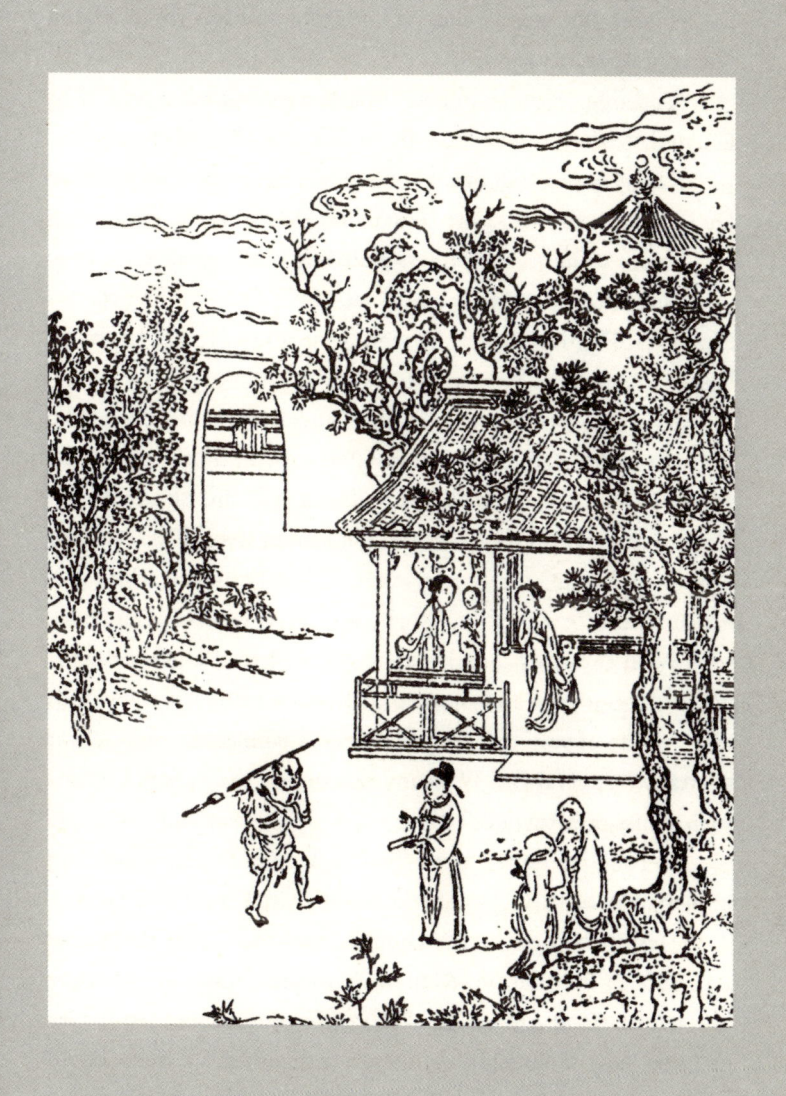

chieftain said. Then, as promised, he withdrew his troops to a reasonable distance from the temple.

The abbot went inside the temple and informed Zhang Sheng of what had happened.

"Although they've pulled back, if we don't hand over Miss Cui in three days, none of us will live," the abbot told him.

Zhang Sheng told the abbot and Madame Cui that his friend Du Que, also known as the General on White Horse, led a troop of a hundred thousand soldiers guarding the Puguan Pass. If he could get a letter to him, the General would come to their rescue. However, Puguan Pass was over twenty kilometers from the besieged temple.

The abbot remarked, "If the General Du comes, we have nothing to fear from Sun Feihu. Don't worry about the letter. I have a disciple named Huiming. He is rash and often takes to alcohol and fighting. If I were to ask him to deliver the letter as a favor, he would surely refuse me. But if I challenge him and explain the difficulty of the task, he will surely want to attempt it."

With these words, the abbot turned to the gathering of people around him and shouted, "I have an extremely dangerous task for one of you: to break the bandit encirclement and deliver a letter to General Du. Who among you has the guts to attempt such a mission? Anyone?"

Before he could even finish his sentence, Huiming immediately rushed forward and yelled, "Me! Let me do it!"

Despite being a monk, Huiming had no interest in reciting scripture or meditation. Rather, he was interested in weapons like sword, spear and cudgel. What's more, he would never give up in the face of hardship. A mission such as this, where he could put his heroism on display, was just what he had been waiting for. After getting the details from the abbot and Zhang Sheng, he told them that they need to do nothing but await his good news.

Huiming tucked the letter away, picked up a broad sword, and strode out of the temple. A couple of soldiers standing guard gate yelled at him to get back, but he whirled the broadsword in such a dazzling display of swordsmanship that the guards cowered back and allowed him to walk past. Huiming then made a dash for Puguan Pass, where he presented the letter to General Du. The letter described the dangerous situation at the temple and asked for a speedy rescue. Zhang had written that such an act would be in accordance with the emperor's expectation that it was the soldier's responsibility to save the common people from calamity.

For a high-ranking general like Du Que, mobilizing troops without an explicit order from the imperial court was a move that could carry serious consequences. However, Zhang Sheng had been his best friend from childhood, and he could not stand idly by while such a friend was in trouble. Moreover, he reflected, it was his inherent responsibility to save ordinary people from peril, and a righteous act of bravery at that.

As the saying goes, a general at the front can refuse even the emperor's order. Despite not having an imperial order to dispatch his troops, Du Que immediately set out with an army of five thousand men, and arrived at the temple that very night.

Though equal in number, Sun Feihu's mob of bandits was no match for the disciplined and highly trained soldiers of the General Du. The chieftain was quickly captured and the leaderless bandits defeated and fled into the wilderness.

CHAPTER IV

The General Du won an unparalleled victory. Zhang Sheng, the abbot and Madame Cui came to express their gratitude. The general bowed to the old lady and apologized that the initial negligence of his troops had led to her being forced into such a predicament by the bandits. Zhang Sheng related to Du Que his story since arriving at the temple: how he had fallen in love with Yingying at first sight, rented a room to stay near her, and finally how he had been promised her hand in marriage for finding a way to repel the bandits. Thanks to the general, everyone was safe once again and Zhang Sheng could marry the love of his life.

Du Que was well aware of Zhang Sheng's worthiness as a husband for the late Prime Minister's daughter and felt sincere happiness for his friend's newfound joy.

"An auspicious event such as this calls for a great celebration!" he said.

"Prepare a feast in honor of the General Du and his bravery!" Madame Cui ordered her servants.

"Thank you, Madame. Yingying is a well-born and virtuous girl from noble blood. Zhang Sheng is a gifted gentleman scholar w hose plan succeeded in repelling the bandits. I sincerely hope that you will honor your public promise to give him your daughter's hand in marriage. I would love to remain and celebrate such a happy occasion with all of you, but my soldiers await me. I shall return later to bestow my congratulations upon the happy newlyweds."

And with that, the general rode off to lead his troops back to Puguan Pass.

Madame Cui expressed her deep gratitude to Zhang Sheng and asked him to move into the study in the western chamber, then invited him to a dinner to be held in his honor the next day.

Hearing this, Zhang Sheng's heart jumped and he could hardly contain his excitement. He barely slept a wink all night.

The next morning he put on a brand-new set of clothes he had been saving, and waited in anxious anticipation, each minute seeming to drag into hours and each hour lasting days. He made infinite adjustments to his clothing, checking again and again to make sure everything appeared its best. Finally, Madame Cui sent Hongniang to invite the young scholar for dinner.

When she entered the room and they exchanged greetings, he pretended that he hadn't been expecting her by asking.

"May I kindly ask what brings you to my quarters?"

"Madame Cui has prepared a dinner for you and asks if you would honor her with your presence. Do please go."

"Of course, of course, I will go. And will Ying ying be attending?"

"The dinner is in recognition of you and your deliverance of us all from certain calamity. There will be no other guests, not even the abbot. Madame wishes to arrange for the marriage between you and Miss Yingying."

Zhang Sheng was beside himself with joy and began to talk incoherently.

"Thank the gods! Thank the gods!" he kept repeating to himself.

Then, turning to Hongniang, he said, "I don't have a mirror with me. How do I look?"

"You look great! Dressed like a true bridegroom. That outfit is so gleaming I can barely keep my eyes open. Flies would slip off a robe so polished and lustrous like yours."

"I never dreamed that a sheer coincidental meeting with Yingying could actually end in marriage! I can now honestly say that marriages such as this are predestined by fate."

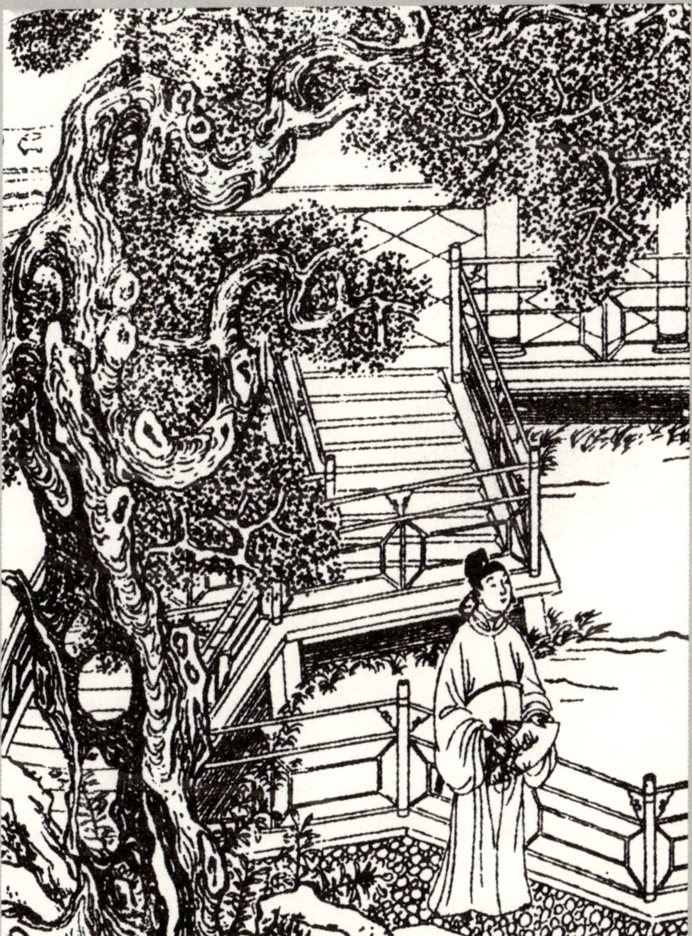

THE ROMANCE OF THE WESTERN CHAMBER

"Yes, husband and wife are brought together by destiny – nothing can stop fate." Hongniang replied.

"But I am just a wandering scholar and have no great dowry for the lady. What shall I do?"

"Miss Cui loves you, not your dowry. Everyone can clearly see how educated and knowledgeable you are. Your bravery saved the Cui family and everyone in the temple. This is the finest dowry Miss Cui could ever hope for. I have already prepared the bridal bed, draped with curtains finely embroidered with two mandarin ducks[1]. Don't you worry about the dowry. All you need to do is to show up."

Hearing this, Zhang Sheng could not help but smile to himself.

"Please go first. I'll be there in a moment after I tidy up my room," he told her.

Upon arriving at the dinner, Zhang Sheng bowed deeply to Madame Cui.

"If not for your heroic action, my family would all have perished at the hands of those horrific bandits. This dinner may be meager, but know that it represents our profound gratitude," she told him.

"It was the good luck you brought to the temple that allowed us to defeat the bandits, dear Madame. Of course, we must thank General Du and his brave troops. Without them, no one in the temple would have survived. Now that these troubles have passed, please let us forget they ever happened," he replied.

Madame ordered her servant to fill Zhang Sheng's cup with wine. Zhang Sheng held up his cup, toasted Madame Cui, and emptied it. Then he refilled it, toasted again to her good health, and again downed the whole cup. Madame Cui merely sipped at

---
[1] A metaphor for an affectionate couple

her cup and then asked Hongniang to bring Yingying in to dinner.

Hongniang went to Yingying's room and bid the young lady to come join her mother at dinner. Yingying had been waiting for this moment, but when it finally came she was overcome by a sudden shyness.

"Who is at the table now?" she asked in feigned ignorance.

"No strangers, just your mother and Scholar Zhang."

"I'm suddenly feeling slightly ill. Please tell them I can't come."

Hongniang noticed that Yingying was constantly sizing herself up in the mirror as she spoke of her sudden 'illness'. She began to tease her.

"Well, if you're not feeling well, just lie down and rest. I'll tell them that you won't be joining them."

"Wait! I… I think perhaps it'd be better if I at least go and have a quick look."

Yingying took another long look at herself in the mirror, bringing a knowing smile to Hongniang's face.

"Dear sister, you are a beautiful young lady. Scholar Zhang is beyond happiness to have you for his wife! Now hurry along, or that foolish scholar will grow impatient."

Yingying left her room and approached the dinner table with a coy smile on her face, her ivory white skin shining brilliantly. Upon seeing her enter, Zhang Sheng felt as if he was in a dream, before Madame Cui's words abruptly awoke him.

"My child, come and bow to your brother."

Zhang Sheng's heart sunk. He knew what this meant - things had taken a sudden turn for the worse. But he couldn't open his mouth. Hongniang was completely taken aback, and thought she could have misheard her mother. Madame Cui's words stopped Yingying in her tracks. She knew how her mother was and realized she had already made up her mind not to honor her promise.

Seeing Yingying standing there dumbfounded, Madame Cui urged her on, "Come along, my dear child. Make a toast to your kind brother."

Yingying felt as if she was lost in a mist, unaware of even her hands that help up the cup in a toast. Zhang Sheng shrank into his chair, not knowing what to say. He drank down the cup Yingying handed him, but didn't taste a thing. Yingying found him pitiable and pathetic. The atmosphere had suddenly become icy cold.

None of this escaped Madame Cui. She knew what they were thinking and how terrible her daughter must feel. But she had made up her mind.

"Hongniang, the Mademoiselle is not feeling well. Take her back to her room and help her rest," she ordered.

After Yingying left, Zhang Sheng turned to Madame Cui.

"Please excuse me Madame, I am not much of a drinker and must say goodbye and take my leave now. But first, I must ask you something. When the bandits besieged the temple you made a promise in front of everyone that whosoever could defeat the bandits would have Yingying as his wife. I came forward, summoned the general, and saved everyone from certain disaster. I had thought that you would keep your promise and approve my marriage to your daughter this very night. Yet, you ask that I call her my sister and she call me her brother?"

"Zhang Sheng, you did indeed save us from the calamity. But my deceased husband had betrothed Yingying to my nephew Zheng Heng. We came to the temple to stay only a short time, waiting for Scholar Zheng Heng to come escort the late Prime Minister's coffin and us back to our hometown. If I allowed you to wed Yingying, what would I tell Scholar Zheng Heng? You'll receive my gratitude in gold and silver and marry a girl. You're

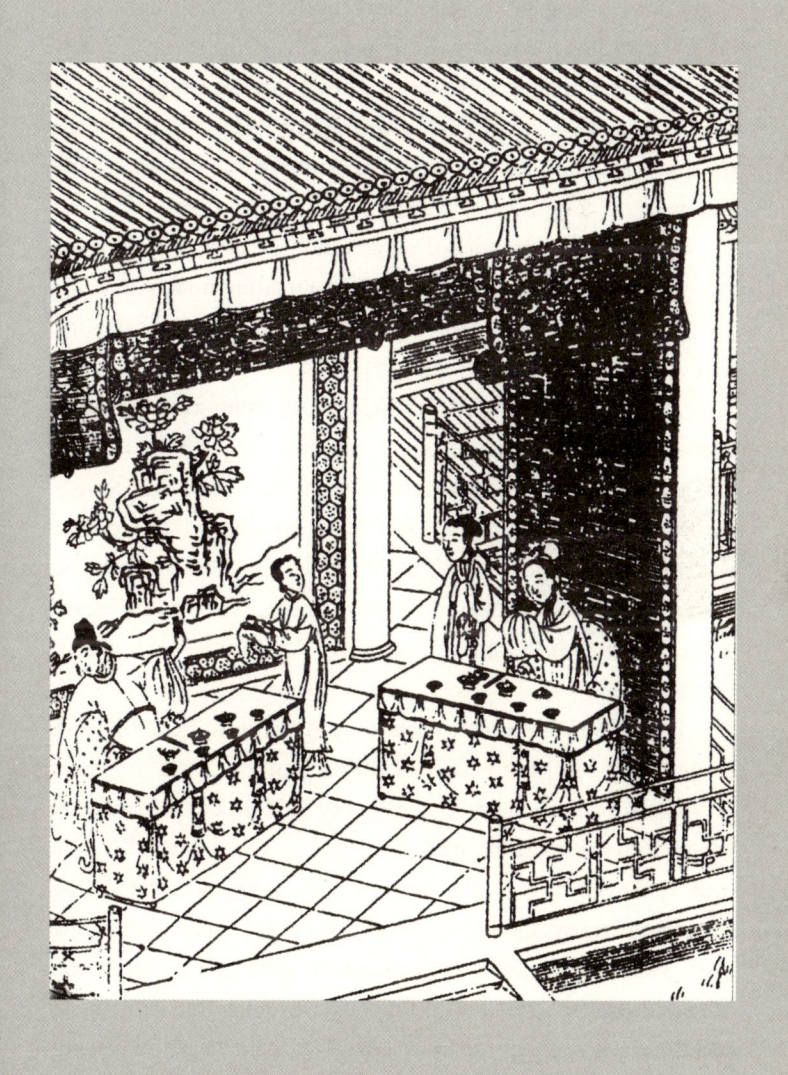

such a talented and handsome young gentleman who won't have any trouble finding a well-matched girl to make your wife."

Zhang Sheng felt the rage slowly boiling up in his stomach.

"I care not for your gold or your silver! As you are clearly determined to break your promise, I must bid my farewell."

Sensing that she was in the wrong and seeing Zhang Sheng's rising anger, Madame Cui loudly announced that he was drunk and ordered Hongniang to help him back to his room.

Zhang Sheng plodded slowly back to his room. Though she felt sorry for him, Hongniang couldn't help but reproach him.

"Just look how sauced you are. If you can't handle alcohol, then maybe you shouldn't drink so much!"

"I'm not the least bit drunk – my current state is from a broken heart. Yingying and I were in love at first sight. When she was in danger, I called the general to rescue her. I had thought our marriage would be announced tonight, and went to this dinner with my heart in the clouds. But Madame changed her mind, and has ground my heart into the dirt. How can she separate us so? Who can possibly fathom my suffering? Who knows such pain as I do now?"

Zhang Sheng's laments went on and on. Seeing him like this, Hongniang felt pity and tried to comfort him.

"I understand that you're suffering terribly, but just imagine what Yingying must be going through as well. Listen, I have a plan. I see you have a lute there, and no doubt you're a skilled musician. Yingying loves the sound of the lute. Tonight, when she goes into the garden to burn incense, you will be waiting on the other side of the garden wall. I'll cough to signal that she's there, and then you can express how you feel in your heart by playing the lute. She will understand."

CHAPTER V

As the night wore on and the moon rose above the willow trees, Hongniang reminded Yingying to burn some incense in the garden. But the young lady was so despondent she sighed lonesomely.

"Incense! What's the use of burning incense?"

"My lady, you've been so devout. What's with the sudden disrespect for piety? A prayer made in sincerity will always have its reward."

"You silly girl, what do you know of these things? Good things don't necessarily happen to good people."

Hongniang burst into laughter.

"Oh please, save your philosophizing for someone else. Come on, let's go."

When they entered the garden a soft breeze was blowing and the tranquil moonlight shone brightly onto the ground as if scattering a thin layer of frost. The garden was empty except for the two young women and their shadows. The seeming desolation of the scene only served to increase Yingying's melancholy as she slowly lit a stick of incense. Hongniang coughed loudly, and suddenly the garden was filled with the melodious sound of lute music coming from beyond the wall. The music sounded like pieces of jade jingling together, bells ringing from a distant tower, or water drops falling into copper kettles.

When the music reached its crescendo, the listener heard angry waves crashing against the rocky shore and flying cranes wailing in the sky. At its nadir, one heard a children's whisper or a lover's whimper. Enveloped in the music, Yingying stood motionless, her emotions moving in tune with the sounds of the lute. She felt as if she dissolved in place and forgot everything around her. Hongniang noticed her state and called her name several times, but Yingying didn't answer, not even knowing that she was there.

THE ROMANCE OF THE WESTERN CHAMBER

The musician started to play another tune, A Phoenix Woos His Mate, first performed by an ancient scholar when he pursued his true love. Soon afterward she heard a poem chanted to the same tune:

My mind lingers on the beauty I saw the other day.
She took my heart at the very first sight.
The phoenix flies around the world in pursuit of its love.
Pity that the lady is nowhere to be found.
I sing my longing through the string of the lute.
When will you be mine and my helplessness come to an end?
When will you promise your love and our hands be joined?
If we cannot soar together, my life will end in vain.

The music and the poem were so imbued with sorrow and despair that Yingying was reduced to tears. She then heard a deep sigh coming from the other side of the wall.

"The mother was ungrateful, while the daughter was telling lies. Gods in Heaven! Why must I suffer such misfortune?"

Yingying then knew that the lute player was none other than the one who had saved her life and to whom her mother had promised her as his wife. In her despair, Yingying could only speak to him in her heart.

"You wrongly accuse me! My mother is the one who changed her mind and broke her promise; I did not lie but her. My heart knows to whom it belongs, but I cannot disobey my mother. There is nothing I can do. If it were up to me, I would have gone with you a long time ago."

Just as Yingying was so immersed in the music and couldn't get out of it, Hongniang came over and had to stir her from the daze the music had induced.

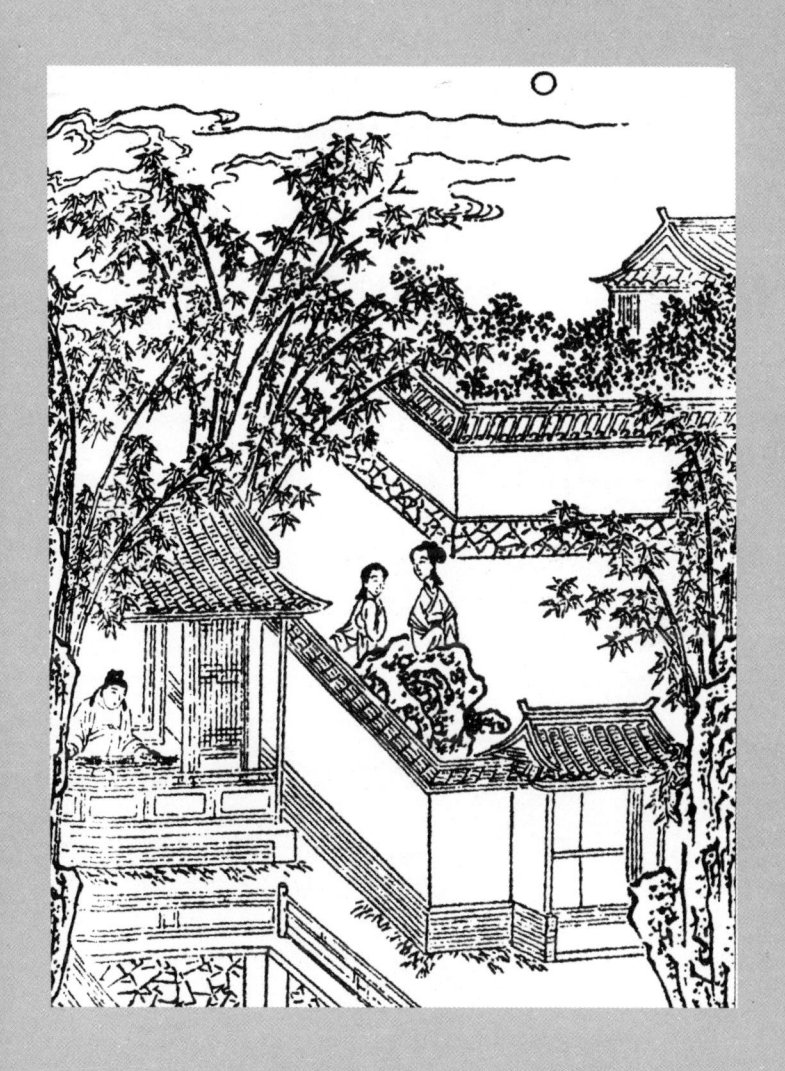

"Your mother is looking for you, my lady. Let's head back."

One the way back to their rooms, Hongniang turned to Yingying.

"My dear lady, what good is it only listening to his music? Scholar Zhang is preparing to leave the temple soon."

"Who told you this?" Yingying asked in shock.

"Scholar Zhang asked me personally to tell you so."

"Then you must go to him immediately and tell him to stay a little while longer."

"And for what?" Hongniang asked mischievously.

"Never mind why, just go!"

CHAPTER VI

The melancholy memory of the lute's music left Yingying with no appetite. She simply sat there sighing and groaning throughout the day. Zhang Sheng was tortured as well. After he finished playing he returned to his room and was left to heartbrokenly consider a future without Yingying. With this on his mind, as well as the chill he caught while out in the garden, he fell seriously ill. When Yingying heard he was sick, she called Hongniang over.

"I have a favor to ask of you. Scholar Zhang is seriously ill. Would you please go visit him for me? While you're there, ask him if he has anything to say to me."

"I can't go, my lady. If Madame found out about this, she'll surely lay the blame on me."

"Please, I'm asking you sincerely, my dear sister."

"I just can't, this is serious. If something happened or someone discovered I was there, I would be in big trouble and wouldn't have any way out of it. I won't go."

Yingying bowed low to the ground, "Please, sister, go for me."

Hongniang smiled, "Enough, enough. I'll go, but only for you. And what do you wish me to say when I see him?"

Yingying had no reply to this question.

Hongniang thought for a moment and said, "When I get there I'll say something like this: my young mistress is also ill. Misery loves company. You should tell her what's on your mind; if the two of you share the same feelings, then you should both recover in no time."

"Who told you to tell him this? Just go have a look and hear what he has to say, then come back and tell me."

Hongniang left for the reading rooms of the western chamber where Zhang Sheng stayed. She didn't knock the door,

THE ROMANCE OF THE WESTERN CHAMBER

but instead walked up to the window and poked a small hole through the window paper with her finger, to first see what he was doing in his room. Through the small hole, she saw Zhang Sheng lying still in bed, fully dressed. The quilt and all his clothes were badly wrinkled, indicating the young bachelor had no one to look after him. When she saw his face, all pale and sunken from fever, she felt sorry for him and blamed it all on Madame Cui for breaking her promise and separating the two young lovers.

Hongniang gave the door a light knock and then stepped inside. Seeing her, Zhang Sheng felt both happy and grieved. He knew who had sent her, and this knowledge reassured him of Yingying's feelings for him and filled his body with warmth. But he could not be sure how long this warmth would last. Regardless, this sign from Yingying gave him a window into her heart and filled the longing he had felt for her in the past few days. What's more, he immediately began to feel his strength recover.

Seeing Zhang Sheng looking so sick, Hongniang advised him to see a doctor.

"No doctor can cure my illness. Madame Cui broke her promise, and now I suffer a broken heart. If I should now die, it shall be from unfulfilled desire. How is Yingying now?"

"My young mistress is not well. She fell ill upon hearing the news of your fever. I hope you won't blame her, she has her own affliction talk and is a victim, too."

"Please, if you have pity for me, you must help me. I want to write a letter for you to take to your mistress."

"I can't, she may fall out with me if I take back a letter. She'll scold me for my recklessness and destroy the letter, and then what would you do?

Zhang Sheng implored Hongniang to help in this simple task, promising her money and silk for her kindness.

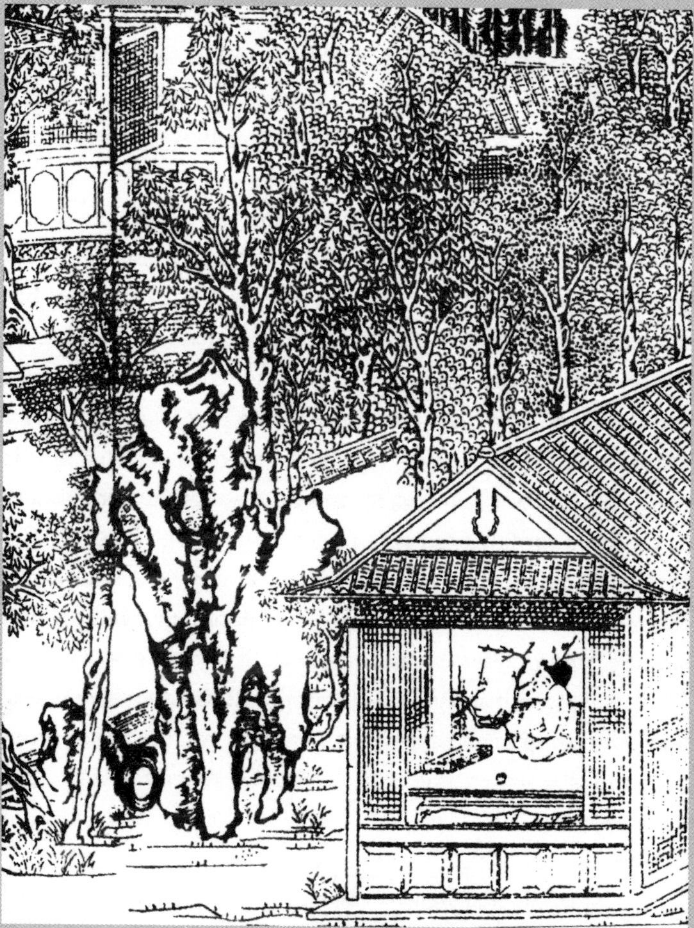

THE ROMANCE OF THE WESTERN CHAMBER

"Though I am a young girl like me ignorant of the world I have no desire for your treasures. However, you saved her life and for this I'm grateful. If it can help alleviate your grief, I'll take the risk for you. Now, put your brush pen to paper and I'll take care of the delivery."

Zhang Sheng was immediately cheered by these words. He soon finished his letter and a poem to go along with it.

"Finished already? You're quite a speedy scribbler. What'd you write? Read it out to me."

Zhang Sheng began reading, "This letter is from Zhang Sheng who presents his regards to Miss Cui. I have not heard from you since our parting the other day, and since then my heart has been filled with sorrow and indignation. Madame Cui rewarded my good deed with a broken pledge. I was forced to surrender the marriage I had been promised, and to part from you. Not a moment passes that I don't miss you, and my only wish now is that I could grow a pair of wings and fly to you at this very instant. But there is nothing I can do – not even speak with you. All I am left to do is pouring out my longing to you onto these empty walls that surround me. These past days I have become very ill, and the sickness only increases as my heart swells for you. Today you sent Hongniang to visit and give me the opportunity to write you a few lines expressing my feelings. If you have pity on me, please write back and give some comfort to this wounded heart of mine." He then read his poem:

With lovesickness growing day by day,
I play the lute thinking away,
Spring comes together with joy,
Can you still silent remain?
Love is not to be refrained,

You should not stand by that praise insincere.
Take a good look at the moonlight,
And my heart is just like the shadow of a flower under your feet.

Hongniang could not exactly understand the meaning of his poem, but she clearly heard its harmony and knew that he was a rather talented young scholar. Furthermore, his show of concern for her mistress will surely warm her heart, and she knew Yingying would be moved upon reading it.

"Don't worry, I'll deliver this letter. Don't be too discouraged – you should put your career first. Get over your broken heart for it will only hurt your future potential."

"Thank you for your kind words, I will never forget about my career."

"Well, I'll go give this to her. Take good care of yourself and wait here for me to bring back some good news."

Zhang Sheng made repeated expressions of his gratitude when seeing Hongniang off. He now regarded her as an angel who could relieve him from this terrible suffering.

Hongniang carefully concealed the letter and went back to Madame Cui's bedroom first, staying there until the Madame went to bed. Knowing that Yingying awaited her, but afraid that she might already be asleep, she tiptoed into her young mistress's room.

When she lifted up the bed drapes she saw her young mistress lying on the bed, her hair in tussles and wearing a long face. Hongniang thought it might be unwise to give her the letter just then, so she left it on the dresser where Yingying would stumble across it on her own.

Just then, Yingying turned over and sat up. got out of bed

and began speaking to Hongniang in an irritated voice, moving over to the dresser to straighten her wild hair. When she reached for the comb she was startled by the sight of the letter, and then noticed Hongniang giggling in the reflection of the mirror. She immediately tore the letter open and read it in a single breath; her face turned scarlet as she began to blush and her heart pounded at the passionate words and fervent lines of poetry.

Yingying considered the letter for a moment, then threw it on the ground and whirled on Hongniang.

"You foolish girl! Who gave you permission to bring this letter to me? I'm the daughter of a distinguished family of the late and noble Prime Minister. How dare you tease me with such a letter! I'll report this to my mother, and she'll teach you how to behave with a good beating. I'll see that your legs broken!"

Hongniang knew her young mistress was bluffing, and she played along.

"Mistress, it was you who sent me to see him. Scholar Zhang asked me to deliver this letter. As I'm illiterate, how could I possible know its contents? I told you I didn't want to go see him, but you forced me to! Now I return with a letter and you want to have my legs broken? Why'd I help you in the first place? Well sister, no need for you to tell Madame Cui, I'll turn myself in and give her the letter."

Hongniang then picked up the letter and headed for the door. Yingying rushed after and grabbed her from behind.

"Wait, wait! I was just kidding, you know…"

"Please let me go." Hongniang said with a pouting face.

"How is Scholar Zhang?"

"I won't tell you anymore of it."

Yingying really believed Hongniang was actually mad at her. She pulled her closer and continued to implore her.

"Please, my good sister, do tell me."

Hongniang wouldn't do so much as to open her mouth. Yingying asked her to sit down and began to try and soothe her.

"You know I was just kidding – we're like sisters, after all. How could I possibly bear to let my mother beat you? Dear sister, please, say something."

Seeing how nervous her young mistress was, Hongniang couldn't keep back a smile. She told Yingying that Zhang Sheng had been thinking of her endlessly, to the point where he couldn't even eat or drink. He simply lay in bed all day, sighing to himself. He was much thinner than before, and whenever he mentioned Yingying his eyes would well with tears. He was in a truly pitiable state.

Yingying sighed, "We should go find a good doctor to look after him."

"Scholar Zhang is afflicted with a broken heart. Medicine cannot help him."

"Hongniang, if it weren't for your sake, I would show my mother this letter to prove this man's worth. But how could he ever face my mother again, having written such things? Yes, he saved our lives and was sorely mistreated, but we're now sworn brother and sister and there can be no other feelings between us. Thank the gods for your good discretion – if someone should find out about this it'd be a disaster."

"Who are you joking? Everyone knows you're the cause of this poor scholar's depression. You're afraid that others will find out that he wrote you that letter and your mother will get wind of it. He was forced to climb the roof and now you've taken away the ladder; what do you expect of him anyways? If you keep this up, he'll really be left with no way out."

"Fine then, I'll write him a letter and let him know he

shouldn't do stuff like this anymore."

Yingying quickly wrote the letter and handed it to Hongniang.

"When you deliver this to Scholar Zhang, tell him that I sent you only because I consider myself his sister and I have no other intentions. If he keeps up with this behavior, I'll have to inform my mother."

Hongniang was confused. She found Yingying's thought process very difficult to follow. There was Scholar Zhang going into fits over her, while she could be ice cold one moment and warm as the sun the next. Who knew when she was saying what she meant. She could be so proper in speech while in front of others but when alone might break down into tears thinking of Scholar Zhang. Hongniang couldn't penetrate her thoughts, but what could she do? She thought of refusing to deliver the letter but she knew she'd be terribly scolded for such insolence. Moreover, she knew poor Scholar Zhang awaited her with baited breath. Finally, she took the letter to his apartments.

Zhang Sheng was elated to see Hongniang return. He bowed repeatedly and obsequiously offered her a place to sit.

"My dear sister, my life depends on you. How did it go? What did she say when she read my letter?" he asked in a trembling voice.

Hongniang had never seen him in such a pitiable state. She knew his happiness would soon melt into despondency once he read her letter.

"Don't be such a fool – she was very angry with your letter."

"How could that be? Did she really read it? Can she be so cruel? If she was angry, it must be that you didn't give her a favorable impression of me."

"How can you say such things? Heaven as my witness, I did

all I could. But she was furious after reading your letter and gave me a terrible scolding. You're the one who wrote that letter and you can only blame yourself – I'm completely innocent in this affair. This is the last time I'll act as messenger and the affection between you two should not extend beyond those of brother and sister. Nothing else. Is that clear? I suggest you cut off your infatuation now and stop whining to me about unrequited love."

Zhang Sheng stood there dumbfounded with his mouth agape at these harsh words.

"Now, the Madame is expecting me. I must go. Good night, Scholar Zhang."

Zhang Sheng fell to his knees and pleaded, "Please! If you don't return, who shall hear my terrible sorrows? My life is in your hands, save me!"

Hongniang shook her head, "You've read too many books. Get this – it's over. Don't expect anything else. The Madame would never assent to such a match. To be honest, I despise the likes of you: you ride on clouds when you're happy then flood the earth with your tears when you're sad. You are both annoying and pitiable at the same time – crazy and foolish one minute and full of sweet words the next. But why am I wasting words? Here, take this letter from my mistress and find out for yourself."

Zhang Sheng grabbed the letter and tore it open. Hongniang prepared herself to see him reduced to pathetic sobs once he finished the letter. But after he finished reading it, she saw that he was beaming with excitement, and repeatedly bowed to Hongniang, each time deeper than the one before.

"This is truly a miracle! Had I known you were bringing a letter such as this, I would have traveled a thousand miles to receive you! Please accept my apologies for not being properly hospitable."

Now Hongniang was really confused.

"You see, it was only a ruse when your mistress scolded me. She's made an appointment with me tonight in this poem she wrote," and he began to read:

Wait till the moon rise over the western chamber,
When a light breeze softly blows open the gate.
The swaying shadow of flowers at the other side of the wall,
Could be the one you are waiting for.

"I didn't hear anything about any appointment," Hongniang said.

Zhang Sheng patiently explained that the poem was an invitation for him to go to the garden after the moon rose and that Yingying would open her door and wait for him there. When she saw the shadows of the flowers dancing in the moonlight, she would know that it was him climbing over the wall to meet her.

Hongniang looked at him doubtfully. "Over the wall? She asked you to climb over the wall? Is she serious?"

"Of course, I've read so much poetry that I know how to interpret a poem such as this."

Hongniang smiled, "I never knew my mistress could be so clever. But you're not the sporting type, how will you get over that steep garden wall?"

"I've seen it twice now – I know what to do."

"But you only stood on the other side reciting poems and playing your lute. Now you've got to jump over it!"

"This poem gives me the determination to overcome any sort of wall. Don't worry – I will do anything for Yingying."

CHAPTER VII

Hongniang returned to Yingying's room. Though she now knew about the secret appointment, she didn't make any mention of it, and rather made a close observation of her young mistress. She noticed that Yingying was dressed different than normal, though she acted the same as always. But Hongniang knew that once evening came and they went into the garden, Yingying wouldn't be able to conceal her intentions any longer.

Hongniang noticed that it was geting dark. "Time to go into the garden and burn incense, my sister," she told Yingying, who merely nodded and said nothing as she followed her into the garden.

The moon-lit garden was deadly silent. A soft breeze carried the fragrance of fresh flowers and new grass.

Yingying turned to Hongniang and said, "It's such a nice evening, if you don't mind I'd like to enjoy it by myself for a short while. Why don't you go back to our room first?"

Feigning ignorance, Hongniang withdrew to the side gate and opened it. When Zhang Sheng saw a dimly-lit figure at the gate, he took it as Yingying's cue and stepped forward, wrapping her in his arms.

Hongniang was furious, "You silly fool! Take a good look – what if Madame had opened the gate and not me?"

Zhang Sheng apologized profusely, "My sincerest apologies! Please forgive my rashness. But where is the young lady?"

"She's by the pond over in the garden. But let me clarify, did she really make an appointment with you tonight?"

"Of course – it's right there in the poem. I couldn't have misinterpreted it."

"Don't go through the gate then, or else everyone will know that I let you in. She wanted you to climb over the wall, so climb you must. It's a clear night and I think the gods may be on your side."

With surprising dexterity, Zhang Sheng scrambled up and over the wall. Once in the garden, he immediately embraced Yingying before she knew what had happened.

"Who is it?" she asked.

"It's me, Zhang Sheng."

This sudden move had caught Yingying off guard. She didn't know what to make of it; after all, she was from a noble family, and though she had some feelings for Zhang Sheng, she couldn't condone this reckless expression of physical affection.

Ashamed and angry, she turned on him and growled "Zhang Sheng! Who on earth do you think you are? I'm here to make an incense offering, and how dare you trespass over the wall? What is it that you're after? What if my mother learned of this?"

Zhang Sheng's enthusiasm deflated immediately – he hadn't in the least expected such a reaction from Yingying. He told himself that it was her who had asked him to scale the wall and meet her in the garden, yet now she was acting all surprised. One look at her cold, moon-lit expression both repelled him and struck him with awe. He simply stood there stupefied, unable to mutter a word in response.

Worried about how things would develop, Hongniang hadn't strayed far. Suddenly, she heard Yingying cry out, "Hongniang, help! There's a thief in the garden!"

She stepped forward and asked in a surprised voice, "Who's there?"

"It's me, Zhang Sheng."

"And whatever are you doing here?" she asked in feigned amazement.

"Take him to Madame! She'll teach him proper etiquette in

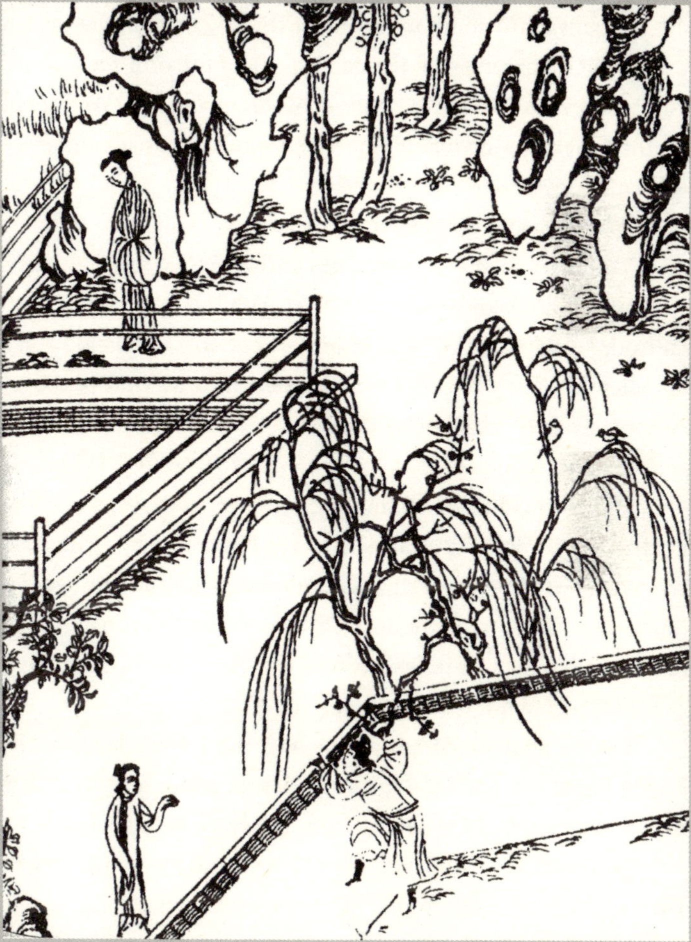

dealing with a lady!"

Now Hongniang was confused too. She thought that Zhang Sheng must have misunderstood the poem's meaning, so she started with a new plan.

"You want to admit to meeting Scholar Zhang in the garden this late at night? Imagine the consequences for your reputation! Not to say what Madame will think of this gentleman. We should do the trial and sentencing ourselves. Scholar Zhang, come here and kneel down!"

Zhang Sheng complied immediately.

"You have read so many books written by the ancient sages, yet you still don't know how to behave. Why are you here at such an hour? You're well educated and ought to be sensible – it's unbelievable that you could be so carried away by your passions! Are you aware of what you've done?"

"I'm not…"

"Now you're really testing my patience. You broke into the garden late at night, in clear defiance of basic etiquette. Scholars can't act like this – you're supposed to pursue a distinguished and illustrious career, are you not? Yet you've turned yourself into nothing more than a sneaky "deflowering thief", a lady killer. How can you pretend not to know your crime?"

Both embarrassed and indignant, the normally eloquent Zhang Sheng was reduced to wordlessness. He only wished that the earth would fracture beneath him and swallow him whole.

Seeing his pitiful demeanor, Hongniang now turned to Yingying, "Please Miss, forgive this man, for my sake."

Yingying said, "If it weren't for Hongniang, I would definitely send you to Madame for disciplining. Then you wouldn't even be able to face your own family and friends. Stand up. We are thankful for your rescue of us and shall make it up to you – but we are sworn siblings, how can you think otherwise? What if my mother knew of this? You shouldn't do such foolish things. If I find you getting up to this again, I won't let you off so easily."

Zhang thought to himself that it was she who asked him to come over, how did it turn out like this, with him taking all the blame? But he didn't dare speak out what was on his mind, and only swore that he wouldn't make such a mistake again.

Yingying scolded him a bit more and began to walk away. Before Hongniang joined, Yingying rubbed her cheek with one of her fingers, making a traditional Chinese gesture of shaming someone.

"Aren't you ashamed," she asked Zhang Sheng.

Zhang Sheng couldn't fathom how it all turned out like this. He was completely humiliated after Yingying's ridicule. Ashamed and angry, he immediately felt his health worsening once he returned to his room.

He has been in a deep slumber lethargically all day, unable to eat anything. The doctor came and gave him some medicine, but it had no effect and his condition worsened. Madame heard of his illness and sent Hongniang to take a look at him and inquire what medicine he took, adding that she would find an imperial doctor to come and diagnose him. Hongniang related all this to Yingying.

Ever since that night in the garden, Yingying had been wracked with guilt. Upon hearing of his illness, she became even more anxious. She pressed Hongniang for details, but the latter told her that even the doctor couldn't make heads or tails of it, though he did say that Zhang Sheng was terribly ill and might not recover. These words caused tears to well up in Yingying's eyes, and she knew she was at fault. She was the cause of this illness and might be the only cure for it.

She told Hongniang, "I know of a folk prescription that

THE ROMANCE OF THE WESTERN CHAMBER

might help him. I'll write it down and you take it to him – don't let anyone else see it."

"Oh, my sister. Please have some mercy on him. Is this prescription of yours a real medicine, or is it yet more of a poison?"

"Rest assured, this is the real deal."

"If it could save his life, then I'll take it to him."

After she wrote down the "prescription", Yingying again warned that no one else was to see it. Hongniang didn't quite understand what all the precautions were for, but she took Yingying's confidence in the remedy as an indication of its efficacy, and she scurried over to give it to Zhang Sheng.

The sight of him truly shocked her. What once a handsome young scholar was now a pale and emaciated skeleton of a man who might be blown over by the slightest breeze.

"How did you come to this condition so quickly?" she asked.

"I'm afraid these are my last days and I shan't see you again.

Just remember the role you've played in my death."

"This world has seen many lovesick people, but none of them as ridiculous and foolish as yourself."

"I saved many lives, yet my own life is taken. The old proverb says about the infatuated women and disloyal men. But for me, it is just the opposite."

"Don't you worry. Madame has sent me to inquire what other medicine you might need. And my mistress has written down a remedy meant only for you."

At this, Zhang Sheng rose up in excitement, "Where is this remedy?"

"It's quite complicated, there are several ingredients that have to be mixed together just so. It goes like this: sweet-scented osmanthus flowers swinging their shadows late at night while the 'angelica' is immersed in vinegar."

Zhang Sheng replied, "Osmanthus flower is 'warm-natured' and angelica is used for promoting circulation of the blood. How can these two be mixed together?"

Hongniang continued reading, "This remedy is most difficult to create for the ingredients are hidden away in obscure corners by the lake and rockery. You may take one or two doses as you like."

"Are there any contraindications?"

"Yes, the contraindications say that 'anemarrhena' is not yet asleep and fears that 'Ladybird' would make a scene. If you feel better after administering one or two doses, you should take 'quisqualis indica' and a little bit of ginseng."

"Did Yingying write this herself?"

"Yes."

Despite his frail state, Zhang Sheng could not help but to burst into laughter. Now he understood everything, though it was clear that Hongniang didn't know a thing about all these strange ingredients. Therefore, she couldn't know that they had nothing to do with his illness. Yingying's "prescription" was actually telling him to meet her late that night but she was afraid her mother might still be awake and that Hongniang might mess things up.[2] She was telling Zhang Sheng that if his love was true, his wish could still be fulfilled.

Zhang Sheng said, "My dear friend, would you believe that your mistress is writing to set up another meeting with me?"

"You silly bookworm! You're reading too much into it again. Didn't you learn your lesson last time?

"But look, there is a poem in the letter – let me decipher it for you."

---

[2] Many ingredients in Chinese traditional medicine have the names that can also be used to refer to people and things in daily life. In Yingying's "prescription", "osmanthus flowers" indicates the season of fall, "vinegar" refers to Zhang Sheng who was poor and pedantic. and the Chinese name for "angelica" name literally means "time for going back home", indicating the hour of their meeting. As for the warnings, there are also four ingredients. The Chinese name of "anemarrhena" literally means "knowing the mother", that of "ladybird" is "Hongniang", that of "quisqualis indica" means "son of a gentleman", and ginseng in China stands for "full recovery".

THE ROMANCE OF THE WESTERN CHAMBER

Disturbed not by these idle things,
Wasted not your god-given talent.
You realized my order and protected me,
Yet never thought this predicted disaster for you.
It's hard for me to trade my love for etiquette
And I will give you this letter as a token of love.
I'll follow the ancients in their deeds rather than their poems
And meet you tonight to fulfill our dream of love.

Zhang Sheng understood the meaning of this poem clearly. Yingying would visit and spend the night together with him. This is the ultimate cure for his illness. Already, he felt almost fully recovered.

Now knowing the meaning of her mistress' letter, Hongniang said to him, "This is great news for you two. But you look so poor and humble and your bed is not presentable. Just look at this shabby old quilt and the lute you use as your pillow? Do you think my delicate lady can sleep on this? How could you both enjoy the night if you're freezing cold?"

"You've got a point – my place is indeed shabby. Look, I've got some silver taels here. Can I buy a set of bedding from you?"

"Nonsense! The pillows and quilts I keep for my lady were made for her wedding night, they're not for sale! But don't worry. I'll make sure that everything is up to her standards."

Zhang Sheng was elated as the prospect of spending the night with his true love. However, he couldn't help but worry about her mother's oversight and the possibility that she somehow might foil their plan.

Hongniang told him, "It all depends on the young lady's will; if she wants to come badly enough she'll walk through the walls to get here. From my perspective, it looks like she's pretty serious. Don't mess this up!"

CHAPTER VIII

Hongniang returned to her mistress' room. Afraid of being taken in again, she pretended to be unaware of all that had happened.

"How is Scholar Zhang? Did he take the prescription?" Yingying asked.

"He's very ill. I showed him the prescription and he read it."

"Did he say anything afterwards?"

"Nothing. But he became very happy after reading it."

Yingying understood and quickly diverted the conversation.

She told her maid she was tired and wanted to take a short nap.

"Will you go help my mother in her room?" Hongniang nodded. "But do not tell her about the prescription."

"My mistress, get some rest. I'm not that foolish."

After some time had passed Hongniang began to fret. She worried that Zhang would figure out that Miss Cui was lying to him, and how he would hurt if that happened.

"I'll wait until I hear her explanation," she told herself to ease her fears. But as dusk was falling Yingying was still acting as if nothing was going on, causing Hongniang to grow increasingly impatient. Finally, she couldn't take it anymore and asked if Yingying had a plan for the night. But Yingying simply replied that she wished to get a good night's sleep.

"If you go to bed, what will Scholar Zhang do?"

"What are you talking about?" Yingying retorted.

"My dear, do you really want to hurt Scholar Zhang this much? If you go back on your word once more, I'll turn you in and tell Madame that you promised Scholar Zhang a date in your letter."

"Well, you little imp! How dare you threaten me?" Yingying blushed w ith anger, but she agreed to the meet Zhang , and admitted that she was a little bashful.

"There's nothing to be bashful about. When you get there, all you need to do is close your eyes and wait. Hurry up. Madame is asleep."

The two girls went to Zhang's room together, where he was waiting anxiously. Hongniang knocked on the door and told Zhang to take the pillows and quilt.

"The mistress is coming. How are you going to thank me?"

"I will always remember your kindness!" Zhang said with a bow.

Hongniang turned to Yingying and told her to go into the room. "I'll wait for you outside."

"How am I so lucky to be blessed with your company?" Zhang said as Yingying entered the room. "Am I dreaming or are you really here? I am neither powerful nor talented but you are an incarnated fairy descending to the earthly world. I hope we can grow old together."

"Scholar Zhang, you are my savior. I fell in love with you the first time I saw you. I promise to be loyal," Yingying replied shyly. They embraced, each muttering more vows of love.

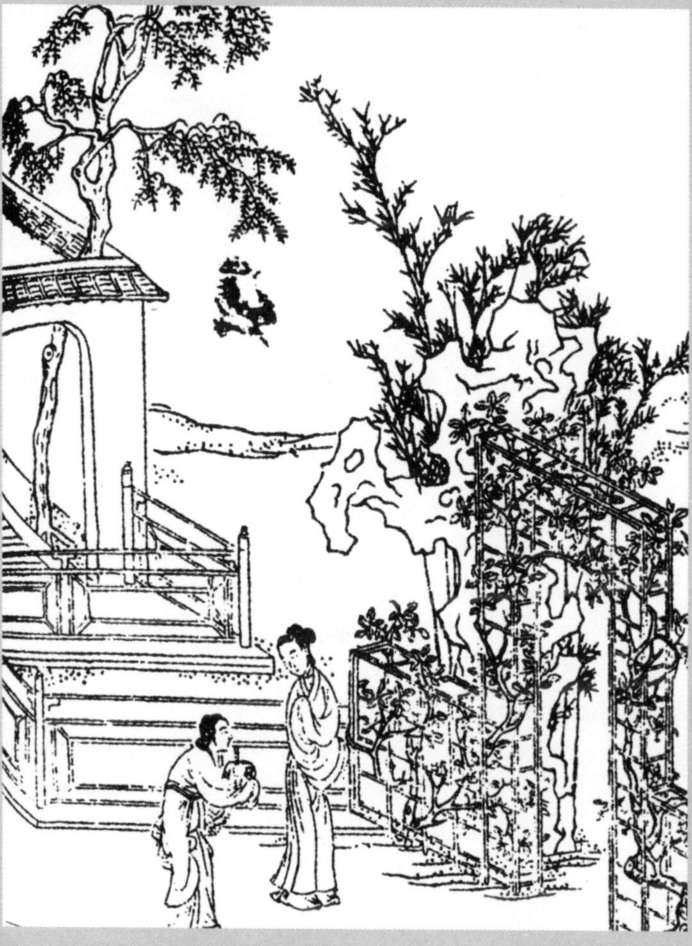

Yingying went to Zhang's room every night after that first one. But it didn't take long for Madame Cui to notice the change in her daughter. Yingying no longer showed any signs of grief, in fact she seemed to be almost joyful. The girl had become absent-minded and lost in her own thoughts. Her manners changed, and there seemed to be different about her body as well. Madame Cui began suspect that something going on between Zhang Sheng and her daughter.

She asked Huang Lang, the page boy, for information, who reported her that Hongniang and Miss Cui had started burning incense in the garden every night. He'd wait for them to come back, but in vain. Guessing what had happened, Madame Cui asked Huang Lang to fetch Hongniang.

Huang Lang rushed to Hongniang and informed her that Madame Cui knew about the nightly incense trips, and warned her that she would most likely receive a beating for that. Hongniang was sacred and ran to Yingying in panic.

"My lady, your mother has found out about the garden trips. She has just summoned me. What do I do?"

"Good sister, you have to help me," Yingying was visibly more scared. "Please cover for me. Just be careful when answering my mother's questions."

"She's going to be angry with me—I was supposed to keep an eye on you. What am I supposed to say when she asks me? You have to help me make up something. I shouldn't be the one to get punished for this! I've done nothing but help you, waiting outside with frozen feet each night, while you and Zhang are locked inside his room. Why should punishment fall upon me?" She stopped to catch her breath and realized there was nothing she could do to escape her fate. "My sister, what's done is done. I'll try my best to cover it up. But if trouble is inevitable, stay calm. After all, she was the one who promised the marriage and she broke the promise. Justice is on our side." She straightened herself up and went to go see Madame Cui.

"You little imp," The Madame yelled at the sight of her. "Kneel down! Don't you know what awful things you did?"

"No, I don't."

"Of course you don't. If you tell me everything today, I will pardon you. But if you dare to lie to me, I will beat you to death. Now speak! Who allowed you to take the Miss to the garden?"

"We have not been to the garden. Who told you that?"

"Huan Lang saw it with his own eyes," Madame Cui pulled back her arm preparing to hit Hongniang.

"Madame, don't hurt you hand. Please be seated. I'll tell you everything. One evening while Miss Cui was finishing her embroidery, we started chatting. I suggested we should pay a visit to Scholar Zhang since he had been sick for such a long time."

"So you went there, well what did he say?"

"He said something about how Madame had mistreated him, and how he'd grown terribly sad. Then he asked me to go back and let Miss Cui stay just a little longer."

"Why?"

"I thought he wanted her to treat him with some sort of magical acupuncture, I never expected that they would become husband and wife. But they've been sleeping together, Madame, for more than a month. They love each other. I think you should let it be. As the proverb says, 'a grown girl cannot be kept at home for long.'"

"You irresponsible girl!" Madame Cui thundered in desperation. "This is all your faults. Why didn't you stop them?"

"It's not my fault, or the Miss's, or Scholar Zhang's. The blame is on you, Madame."

THE ROMANCE OF THE WESTERN CHAMBER

"How can you put this blame on me?"

"Trustworthiness is the most important trait a person can have," answered Hongniang. "Remember when those bandits besieged the temple. Madame, you promised—in front of everyone—that your daughter would marry the person who could fight off the wicked soldiers. Zhang brought troops, defeated the enemy and rescued everyone in the temple. You, however, did not keep your promise. If you didn't want them to get married, you should've asked him to leave with a handsome sum of money. But instead you promised a marriage and then invited him to move here. The two met daily. How could you have stopped them from falling in love? This is your own fault, Madame. What's done is done. If you make this public the family's name would be ruined. Also, what if Scholar Zhang passes the royal examination and is appointed to an official post? Do you think he will stand for this act of ungratefulness? Even if you bring it to the court, you would be charged with not fulfilling your responsibility as head of a family and everyone would know that you rewarded a heroic act with ingratitude. Why not forgive their mistake and accept their marriage? It's in everyone's best interest. The young scholar is talented and your daughter is pretty and graceful, they're a perfect match."

Madame Cui was silenced by these words. She knew Hongniang was right, that the best course of action was to accept it. She sighed deeply.

"Fine! My daughter doesn't deserve another man so let her marry Scholar Zhang. Hongniang, call her in!"

Hongniang ran straight to Yingying who was nervously waiting.

"What happened?"

"I told her everything regardless of the consequence. She was

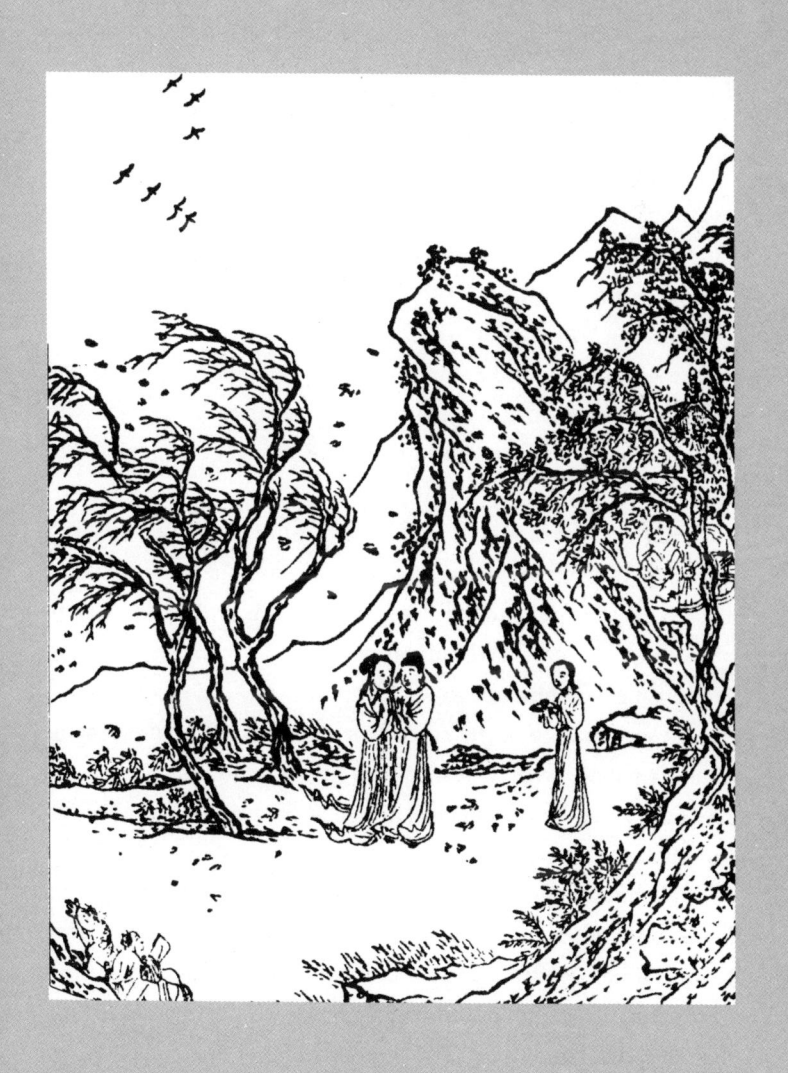

going to find out sooner or later. Now she is waiting for you, and, she's going to say yes to your marriage. Receive my congratulation in advance."

Yingying was happy but still a little worried at the idea of facing her mother.

" What's to be ashamed of in front of your own mother? Where was your sense of shame when you dated Zhang in the evening and slept together?" Yingying blushed and went with Hongjiang to see Madame Cui.

"I never thought you should act like this! A troublemaker! If I sue Zhang Sheng in the court, it would disgrace the reputation of the Cui family and ruin your father's name. Noble families such as ours are not expected to do such things. Forget it! I can only blame my ungrateful daughter. Hongniang, go and fetch that brute!"

Hongniang arr ived at Zhang 's door, and, upon being informed that Madame Cui wanted to see him, he grew nervous. He asked the maid to tell him what had happened and was shocked to learn that Madame Cui had known every thing. Hongniang told him not to worry though, Madame Cui ordered him to see her so that she could betroth Yingying to him. Zhang couldn't believe what he was told so he panicked. The fear on his face has caused Hongniang jeer at him as she pushed him towards the Madame's room.

He bowed nervously in front of Madame Cui, and though he knew Yingyin was standing behind her he dared not raise his eyes to look at her. Madame Cui lectured him for some period of time but eventually she promised that Yingying would be his wife, but there was one condition.

The Cui family had for generations never betrothed daughters to common civilians and, currently, Zhang Sheng was just a Xiucai, one who only passed the imperial examination at the county level and had no official position. She demanded that he attend the royal examination in the capital. If he failed he would not be welcomed back. She ordered him to return to his room and pack for he was to leave the next day.

CHAPTER IX

Madame Cui ordered a farewell dinner to be prepared in the Resting Pavilion. It was late autumn, and although the sky was cloudless, the wind was rustling and the yellow leaves were everywhere. The colors and growing signs of winter gave the evening a note of melancholy. Yingying was sad, knowing that she would be saying goodbye to Zhang in only a few hours. She wished for time to stop.

Though she normally dressed up to see Zhang, this night she decided against it. She put on a casual dress and wore no makeup. Hongniang was surprised to see her young mistress in such a state.

"Why are you dressed so casually, Miss Cui?"

"Women dress themselves up for their lovers, but I am about to bid mine farewell. I don't even know when I will see him again. I've been crying all day, how am I supposed to dress up tonight?" The two girls entered the dining room together. Madame Cui was asking the abbot and Zhang Sheng to take their seats and instructed Hongniang to fill their cups.

"Come closer," she said to Zhang. "You are now a member of the family, so please don't be timid and shy away from others. I already betrothed my daughter to you. You're going to attend the imperial examination in the capital and I'm here to see you off. Your future career has an important bearing on Yingying's happiness. Don't let her down. We hope to welcome a top scholar back."

"Thank you for your trust. I have faith in my ability. I have been studying for many years. I will pass the exam and get a post in the government."

Knowing that Yingying hadn't had her breakfast, Hongniang tried to persuade her to have some soup, but Yingying could not eat. She didn't care about Zhang's rank or wealth, all she wanted was to lead a peaceful and tranquil life with the man she loved.

THE ROMANCE OF THE WESTERN CHAMBER

And she was angry that these were the things that would separate her from Zhang. Zhang felt the same. He sat at the table, keeping his head low to hide his tears. But Yingying, who always paid close attention to him, noticed his sadness.

When dinner was over Madame Cui went back to the temple, and the abbot approached Zhang.

"I'll keep an eye on the results. When you win the first place, you should invite me to dinner for I helped in your marriage. From now on, I'm afraid I won't be able to concentrate on my scriptures or services. I'll be anxious to hear your good news. Take care." He patted Zhang on the arm and then left.

"You don't have to take my mother's words too seriously," Yingying told him when ever yone else had left. "I don't care about your promotion, fame or wealth. What I want is to grow old with you. Whether or not you get the first place or promotion, please just come back as soon as possible." She was starting to question everything: What would happen to her husband after the departure? Would he betray her?

"Have faith in me, Yingying," Zhang swore, as if he could read her thoughts. "I will win first place and present it to you as a wedding gift."

"My dear husband, I have nothing to present you as gift but a poem," she took out a piece of paper and handed it to him.

Left alone, I can't bear recalling
The dearest love cherished by you and me.
Do not repeat to your new sweetheart
Those promises you made to me!

"My love, don't speak like that. My heart belongs to nobody but you," He said hoping to comfort her. "I also have a poem for you."

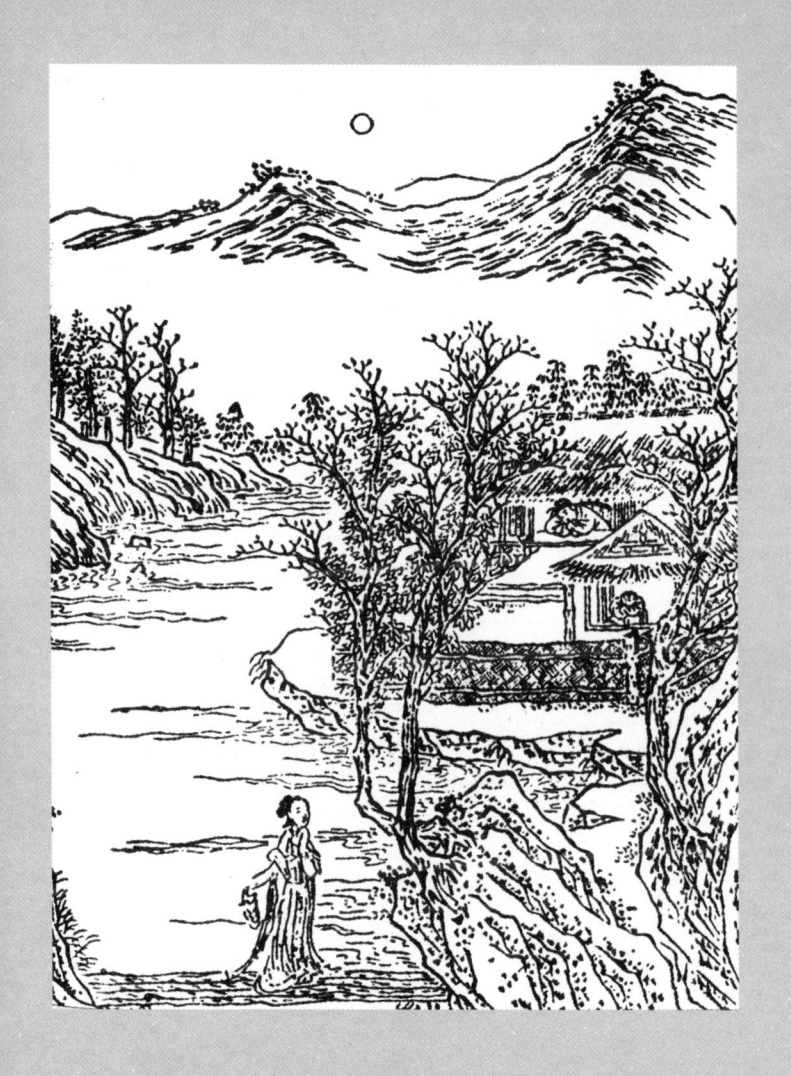

On whom do we depend
In this world full of departures?
To whom do I sing my tune
Except the one sharing with me my heart?

"You will be far from home," Yingying said, trying to stop her tears. "Eat and sleep well. Pay attention to the change of season. You worry about your luck in your career and I worry about your change of heart. Don't leave us in darkness. Write to me often. And don't be carried away by other girls."

"You are the only one that can carry me away," Zhang Sheng replied.

As it grew darker outside, Hongniang finally decided to break apart the mourning couple.

"Madame has returned to the temple," she informed Yingying. "We should head back too."

Zhang bid farewell to Yingying with a sinking heart. The silhouette of his carriage flashed against the setting sun and disappeared among the mountains, leaving Yingying staring at his fading figure, her eyes soaked in tears and heart filled with sorrow.

Zhang had already packed so the carriage quickly took him on the start of his journey. He and his servant stayed at a small hotel in Pudong that night. The bare room only added to his depression.

"I was sleeping on silk last night, and tonight, I'm in a shabby room with broken windows and thread bare blankets. I was with her yesterday, I never foresaw this." He sighed as he fell onto the bed, and exhausted from the day, he was soon asleep. But it was not long before he heard someone knocking at the door. Curious and confused he sleepily went to open the door.

Cui Yingying was standing there before him. Her clothes

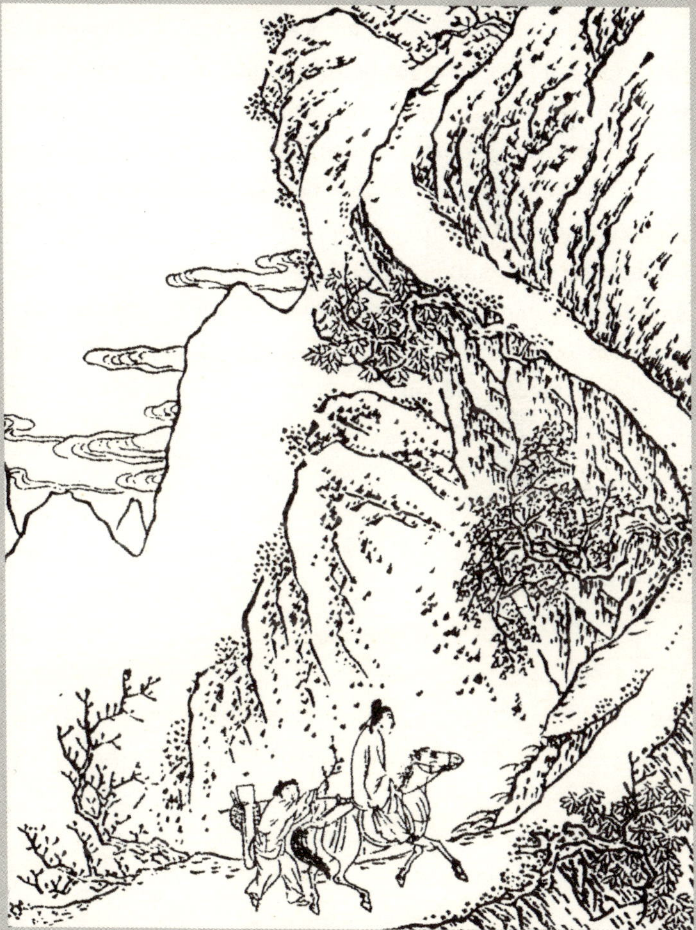

were wet with dews and shoes were covered with mud. Zhang quickly ushered her inside and bent to help her take her shoes off. "I was so worried about you that I snuck out once my mother went to sleep. I want to go with you."

Just as they poured out their hearts, someone was knocking the door. Soldiers on night patrol found Yingying suspicious, who crossed river alone in the small hours of the morning so they chased her all the way to the small inn. Zhang Sheng was surprised to find that Yingying had changed to completely a different person who, instead of whispering her words she became articulate. The overbearing soldiers didn't listen to her regardless of her reasons. As they were about to take her away Zhang Sheng woke up from his dream with a start.

Zhang felt lost and sad.

CHAPTER X

Zhang Sheng arrived at the capital and for six months all he did was preparing for the exam. He had been so busy studying that he'd neglected writing Yingying letters as she had asked him to. His hard work paid off eventually when he won the first place and became the top scholar of the year. He missed Yingying terribly and wanted to return to her immediately and share the good news. However, he had to stay in the capital and wait for the emperor to offer him an official position. Finally he wrote her a letter and gave it to his pageboy, telling him to bring it to the temple as fast as possible.

Meanwhile, Yingying had been miserable for the last six months, and not hearing from Zhang made it exponentially worse. She had become so depressed that she stopped caring about dressing nicely and lost a great deal of weight.

The pageboy finally arrived at the temple with the letter from Zhang. He was taken to Madame Cui in the front hall and reported the good news of Zhang's success on the examination. He then went to see Yingying in the back hall. When Hongniang saw the boy she inquired about Zhang immediately. He told her the same thing he had told Madame Cui that Zhang had won the first place and would soon be appointed a high rank. He told her that Zhang had sent him to the temple to deliver the good news to Miss Cui.

Hongniang nearly skipped into Yingying's bedroom. "Sister, great news! Zhang Sheng is to be offered a government position soon!"

"Don't tease me, if you want to cheer me up," Yingying warned.

"I'm not! The pageboy is outside. He's already reported everything to Madame and now he has come here to give you a letter from your husband."

"Send him in!" Yingying yelled happily.

The boy gave her Zhang's letter, which she read and then reread, not wanting to miss anything. For the first time since his departure she felt relieved. Now she could wait until he received his promotion and then they would marry.

She asked Hongniang to make the pageboy some food, and while they waited she wrote a reply letter to Zhang. She also went about preparing him a care package with some new clothes, a Chinese lute, jade hairpin and a brush. Finally, she gave the pageboy ten silver taels to cover his expenses on the way back.

"Zhang is a government official now and should have had this stuff already, right?" Hongniang asked.

"Not so. Everything here has a special meaning attached to it."

"Really? What do they mean? Please enlighten me."

"The undershirt is worn against his skin, representing the love between us; the scarf is so that he won't forget me; the socks tell him to choose his path carefully; the lute is to remind him of the time we chanted poems and played musical instrument together under the moonlight; the jade hairpin is for him to keep in mind his wife when he puts on an official hat and the writing brush is made of bamboo, w ith each speckle standing for a teardrop to let him know that I've been thinking of him every day." Hongniang nodded in agreement. Yingying then turned to the pageboy. "Can you remember all these words?" He nodded.

"Thank you. Take good care of everything and when you give them to Master Zhang, tell him what each means so that he'll know I do care."

"Yes, Miss."

"And I took special care folding the clothes so don't use this pack as pillow. If you get caught in the rain, don't wring them out.

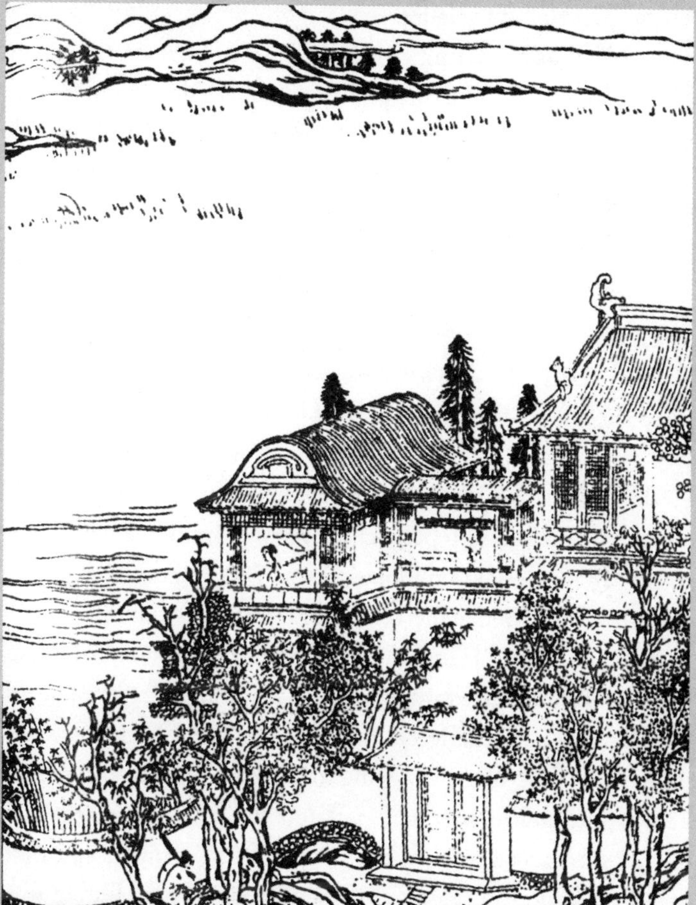

I don't want them wrinkled."

"Of course."

The pageboy soon went on his way. When he returned to the capital he gave Zhang the letter and package from Yingying. Zhang marveled at the letter.

"Her hand writing can match up to that of the great calligraphers now and in the past. Her literary talent is rarely seen in this world." He unwrapped each present from her, guessing the meaning of each before the pageboy could tell him. He praised Yingying's excellent needlework and tenderness. "What else did she say?"

"The young mistress asked me to tell you not to start a new love affair."

"My bride," he said to himself with a shake of his head. "You just don't know what I'm thinking."

He asked the boy to pack up as they were leaving for Hezhong Prefecture, where he would be reunited with Yingying. The two men began to prepare for their departure when Zheng Heng , Madame Cui's nephew whom Yingying was originally betrothed to, arrived at the Temple of Universal Salvation.

When Zheng Heng received Madame Cui's letter he had not been able to leave for the temple immediately. Later he heard that Sun Feihu had besieged the temple, and was intending to do whatever it took to get Yingying to be his wife, even if it meant kidnapping and forcing her. He knew that Zhang brought in a troop of men and rescued the people of the temple; and that finally Madame Cui promised to betroth Yingying to him. It was that last piece of information that made Zheng realize he could not wait any longer.

He arrived at the temple but dared not see his aunt, so he stayed in a small inn nearby. In secret he tracked down Hongniang and invited her to his place, intending to find out information about Yingying before taking action.

"Why have you not visited your aunt?" Hongniang asked him upon her arrival.

"Yingying was originally betrothed to me," he answered. "My aunt knew about this arrangement. If my uncle hadn't died I would be married to Yingying. Now that her mourning has ended, I'm here to plan our wedding. After that I will accompany my aunt and Yingying to bury my uncle in Bolin. Hongniang, I need your help with this. Tell my plan to your lady. When it's done, I will reward you."

Hongniang didn't like Zheng and was angry with him for his secretive arrival.

"Master Zheng," she replied, "You might as well save all that for yourself. Madame Cui has already married the young lady to Master Zhang Sheng."

"Surely you are familiar with the old proverb: 'You can't put two saddles on one horse.' Yingying's father promised her to me, how can her mother change things around? This doesn't make any sense.

"You shouldn't look at it like this. Let me ask you: where were you when that bandit Sun Feihu and his five thousands thugs had surrounded the temple? If it hadn't been for Master Zhang, the entire Cui family would have perished. Who would you marry then? Now that everything's calmed down you think you can just show up and put up a fight for your wedding. If Yingying had been taken by the bandits would you be put up such a fight with them?"

Hongniang's words rendered Zheng Heng completely speechless. He thought for a short time then said, "I would cede Miss Cui if she was betrothed to a wealthy man from a noble family. But she's married to a bookworm dressed in rags! I'm from

THE ROMANCE OF THE WESTERN CHAMBER

a noble family and, what's more, share relations with her. I also have her father's mandate. Besides, everyone knows I'm a better match for her than that loser. Anyway, could he have fought those five thousand bandits by himself? All he did was calling his friend to fight for him. This is ridiculous!"

Hearing this, Hongniang immediately saw the contrast between a gentleman and a base person.

"As for the marriage between Master Zhang and my mistress," she said, "her mother has given full consent with the abbot and General Du as their witnesses. Your quest is a futile one and I suggest you abandon it - the sooner the better."

Zheng Heng was irritated, "Neither the abbot nor the general, and certainly not you, can persuade me to let go so easily. If you want to play games, I'll call over a small army myself to put Yingying in a wedding sedan and bring her to my house. Once I make her my wife and turn her from a girl to a woman, no one can do anything about it."

Hongniang was furious, "You unconscionable person! Despite your noble descent, you're no better than that bandit Sun Feihu! If you dare to make such a move, it'll land you nowhere but prison and even your own family won't be able to help you out."

Having scolded by merely a maid, Zheng Heng was very upset. "You little minx! Looks like that penniless rat has bought you out already. I've got nothing else to say to you but this: I will take Yingying as my wife, heaven as my witness!"

"She will never marry you!"

Zheng Heng decided not to waste any more of his time on Hongniang. He would go straight to his aunt the very next day and pretend not to know of the situation between Yingying and Zhang Sheng. Then he planned to start a rumor about his competitor, telling his aunt that Zhang was married to Minister

Wei's daughter. He knew his aunt could be counted on to believe wild rumors, and besides, his uncle had betrothed him to Yingying and who was his aunt to go back on it? So long as he kept to his guns, he thought, no one would dare stand up to him – especially Yingying.

The next day Zheng Heng went to visit his aunt. She had already heard from Hongniang that Zheng Heng had been asking all about Yingying. Truth be told, Madame Cui was quite fond of Zheng Heng and she had sincerely wished he would become her son-in-law. What's more, the late Prime Minister himself had made that match. Now she had broken her husband's word and his wish. She knew Zheng Heng would come over and question her, but she didn't blame him – the fault all lie with her.

Zheng Heng bowed before his aunt and put on a long face.

"My dear nephew, why didn't you came and see me first upon your arrival?"

"I am ashamed to see you," he replied.

"Alas! We were here waiting for you, but you didn't show up. Then came that terrible Sun Feihu and his frightening bandits. There seemed to be no escape when that young scholar stepped forward with a solution. Because he saved us, I promised him Yingying's hand. I know this isn't fair for you, but please forgive me. Your forgiveness is all I can hope for."

Zheng Heng said in feigned surprise, "I didn't know that's how it happened. What a pity. I had sincerely hoped to become your son-in-law and wait on you. But now it seems impossible to fulfill this wish. By the way, who exactly is this gentleman that you speak of?"

"He's a native of Luoyang, by the name of Zhang Sheng."

Zheng Heng pretended to be shocked when he heard this name. "Zhang Sheng? Which Zhang Sheng, exactly? Can't be the

THE ROMANCE OF THE WESTERN CHAMBER

one who won the first place in the imperial examination?"

Madame Cui could barely conceal her pride. "Yes, that's the one. I didn't expect so much from him. Anyways, he's a good match for my daughter, and she for him."

Zheng Heng let out a long sigh. "Madame, I must tell you. A couple days ago I went to see the list of those with the highest scorers on the examination. I saw this Zhang Sheng's name at the top of the list, from Luoyang and 24 years of age. Since he was the highest scorer, he was to parade through the streets for three days following his official appointment, as is the custom. So that day I joined the crowd to watch the parade. We were waiting at the entrance of Minister Wei's residence, beneath their two-storied archway where Miss Wei, a girl said to be 18 years old, was standing atop to choose her future husband from among the passersby in the parade. As the court officials and newly appointed winner passed by, Miss Wei threw the lucky ball into the procession and struck Zhang Sheng's head directly. Suddenly, a large contingent of maids and servants ran out from the house and pulled him in by force. As this happened, we heard him shout, 'I'm already married. My wife is the daughter of the late Prime Minister Cui.' Wei is a powerful man, and no one paid the poor young scholar any attention. Then the minister told him: 'This grand archway was built by imperial order permitting my daughter to choose her own husband. You cannot defy this order. You will marry my daughter and make Miss Cui to be your concubine. As you and Miss Cui slept together before the official wedding, the marriage is not lawful and she cannot be your wife. You must marry my daughter.' Madame, this was such a scandalous affair that the news spread like wildfire around the capital, so I remember the young man's name very clearly."

Madame Cui's body trembled with anger upon hearing

this story. "Alas, I knew this man would be unappreciative and ungrateful. No wonder he betrayed my poor girl Yingying. How can the daughter of the late Prime Minister be someone's concubine? How embarrassing! Oh, if only I had taken you as my son-in-law. Now I'm full of regret for consenting to their marriage."

"But consented you have. What can you do?"

Madame Cui thought for a moment then said, "Well, since Zhang Sheng had to marry by imperial decree, you should still be my son-in-law, as your uncle arranged it. Don't waste any time – choose an auspicious day for the wedding and make Yingying your wife."

Zheng Heng couldn't help but laugh to himself at how easily Madame Cui had took his story hook, line and sinker.

"I would love to," he said. "But you have promised Zhang Sheng. What if he puts up a fuss when he comes back?"

"How could he dare do so? I'm here as your guarantee. Just pick a date and move here as soon as possible."

Zheng Heng couldn't believe how easily Madam Cui was duped. In his head he was already planning the wedding – meals, tea, gifts and more.

So Madame Cui had changed her mind once again, despite Zhang Sheng's tremendous achievement of finishing first on the imperial examination. The news of Yingying's upcoming marriage to Zheng Heng caused quite a shock to those at the temple. The abbot, for one, was quite doubtful of Zheng Heng's story. He had been cheering for Zhang Sheng throughout the time and waited anxiously for the exam results to be published. He was overjoyed when he saw Zhang Sheng's name at the top of the list. He sent one of his disciples out to inquire about the young scholar's forthcoming official appointment and had learned that He would become a prefecture magistrate – the third highest position in the official hierarchy. Local officials from the surrounding areas were coming to the temple to congratulate him. The General on White Horse also came, who was to preside over the wedding between Zhang Sheng and Yingying. However, Madame Cui refused to participate in the celebration, despite the vexed abbot's urgings.

Having received his appointment as the magistrate for Hezhong prefecture, Zhang Sheng left the capital for the temple in great expectation. He carried the coronet and official robes that Yingying would wear on their wedding day. After greeting the local officials who had come to receive him at the rest pavilion by the road, he galloped straight for the temple. His overflowing joy made it seem as if he was riding on air. Amid the crash of galloping hooves, Zhang Sheng reflected on the events of the past year. Not so long ago he had been just another ordinary scholar; now he was the highest scorer on the imperial examination! His name had been registered with the Imperial Academy for his outstanding scholarship and he was appointed magistrate of a prefecture. His career had progressed leaps and bounds in such a short time. He pictured in his head how happy and proud Madame and Miss Cui would be to see him return in all his glory, and Madame Cui wouldn't be able to look down on him any longer.

Outside the temple he quickly dismounted and went straight in, not even greeting those who were kneeling outside the gate to receive him. He rushed into the chamber where Madame Cui was staying and fell on his knees as any son-in-law would before his future mother-in-law.

"As the declared top candidate of the imperial examination and newly appointed magistrate of Hezhong Prefecture, I am honored to pay my respects to you as your son-in-law."

Zhang Sheng knew that something went wrong when he saw

that Madame Cui didn't even deign to raise her eyes.

"Save it! By imperial decree, you have married the daughter of Minister Wei. I'm below your respect. As the son-in-law of the minister, what are you even doing here?"

Zhang Sheng was taken aback as he had no clue what she was talking about.

Madame Cui continued, "I have only one daughter, Mr. Zhang. Though she might not be called a startling beauty, she was born to the late Prime Minister and is of noble blood. If Sun Feihu hadn't come here with his band of gangsters, you'd never have had a chance with her. You've accomplished much as a scholar and have been appointed a high official, and for this I congratulate you. But then you betrayed the Cui family within a single day! You've got the minister's daughter as your wife and you still want my daughter as your concubine? How dare you!"

Now Zhang Sheng was doubly confused about this misunderstanding but he smelled a rat.

"Dear Madame, I don't know where you heard such slander, but it's all rumors – believe me. I am committed to marrying none other than Yingying. I don't even know who this Minister Wei is, much less his daughter. I've rushed back here from the capital to marry Yingying!"

Madame Cui turned her head and refused to answer.

Zhang Sheng then turned to Hongniang and asked, "How is Yingying?" Hongniang glared at him and replied coldly, "You have no right to ask! You're now the son-in-law of the Wei family and my mistress will marry into the Zheng family. The two of you have nothing to do with each other anymore."

Zhang Sheng again entreated Madame Cui, "Mother-in-law, please, who told you this vicious rumor?"

Madame Cui replied impatiently, "My nephew saw

everything – it must be so."

She repeated the whole fabrication as Hongniang standing by the side, sneering at him with the deepest of contempt and scorn. Zhang Sheng sensed he was in a trap. He swore to heaven that he had never married the Minister's daughter.

"Sister Hongniang," he began. 'You have seen almost all that has happened between Yingying and me. I can understand that others might not believe me, but how can you? Surely, you know all the pains and hardships I have endured for Yingying more than anyone else. I swear to you all that I would rather be struck dead by lightning from heaven than betray my love Yingying."

Hongniang had initially doubted the veracity Zheng Heng's story. She knew Zhang Sheng pretty well from their long acquaintance, and seeing his present sincerity, she felt there must be some foul play.

"Madame Cui, I don't believe Master Zhang is an ungrateful person. Perhaps we should invite your daughter in to ask for herself."

Madame Cui didn't take Zhang Sheng's oath lightly and she began to suspect that there might be something undiscovered going on here. She agreed to Hongniang's suggestion that Yingying be brought into the discussion.

Throughout Zhang's absence, Yingying had experienced the most profound bliss and most abject misery. The news of Zhang's success on the examination had made her ecstatic, but then Zheng Heng's story had completely crushed her. The terrible rumor added to the anxiety produced by her former fiancé's presence. She had spent those days doing nothing but shedding tears and wailing in desperation. When Hongniang showed up to ask if she wished to come in and speak with Master Zhang, she burst into a fit. She longed to see him, but at the same time she hated him. She didn't want to believe the rumor, and meanwhile she couldn't just ignore it. Hongniang repeated to her everything Zhang Sheng had told Madame Cui and suggested she go see him herself and clear things up. Yingying thought for a moment and agreed.

She sat up and didn't bother to change clothes and freshen up. Her face was pale and her hair uncombed, just like a bedridden patient. Assisted by Hongniang she entered Madame Cui's room. At the sight of his haggard bride, Zhang Sheng felt a shock and stabbing pain in his heart. As he stepped forward to greet her, she burst into uncontrollable sobbing.

Zhang Sheng approached her and began speaking. "Since I left you, I had been so busy preparing for the exam that I didn't have time to write. After I got the first place, I sent a messenger here to deliver the good news. I received your gifts and I knew your heart. I have now been appointed a prefecture magistrate by imperial decree and I didn't waste a minute to return to your side. All of these should make you happy, yet you appear crushed. What's happened?"

Yingying replied sharply, "I didn't hear from you for ages! I was ecstatic to hear of your success and anxiously awaited your return. But who would have known that along with you came the news of your marriage by the imperial decree? What have I done to deserve this? How could you betray me and wed the minister's daughter?"

"Calm down, my wife, Heaven will attest to my innocence. My love for you will never alter and I have not betrayed you. Look, I've brought here the items for our wedding. Please don't believe this vicious rumor – I've been framed and I'll get to the bottom of it."

As they were arguing, the abbot returned to the temple with the General on White Horse. General Du had planned to preside over the wedding and didn't expect any more hiccups. Thus, when the abbot told him of the rumor Zheng Heng was spreading and his intent to disrupt the wedding, he was furious. He knew his friend's heart and trusted that he would never betray his true love.

General Du entered the temple and went straight to Madame Cui, declaring, "You once said the Cui family wouldn't take any common scholar as their son-in-law. Well now my brother is the prefecture magistrate, no ordinary accomplishment. What's more, he and Yingying are a perfect match. I didn't expect you to go changing your mind again, but here we are. And why? Anyone can see that Zheng Heng is lying, and his lie can't go on forever. If my brother had actually married by imperial decree, where is his wife? What's more, if this supposed happening was such a big deal in the capital, how is it that nobody else knows about it? Madame, if you still doubt me, why don't we bring in Zheng Heng and question him directly?"

Madame Cui agreed and Zheng Heng was sent for. Already in his wedding clothes, Zheng Heng was on the verge of realizing his plan. But when he saw Zhang Sheng and the general, he knew the jig was up.

He forced out an awkward greeting, "The first place scorer in the imperial exam honors us with his presence. Allow me to give you my sincerest congratulations."

Zhang Sheng asked in a flat voice, "Master Zheng, you said you had witnessed me being married to Minister Wei's daughter. Allow me to ask, where did you see this happen?"

General Du chimed in, "Yes, tell us the details!"

Zheng Heng had nothing to say and could only lower his head in shame.

General Du declared, "You made the whole thing up! You've spread vicious rumors so that you could steal the wife of Zhang

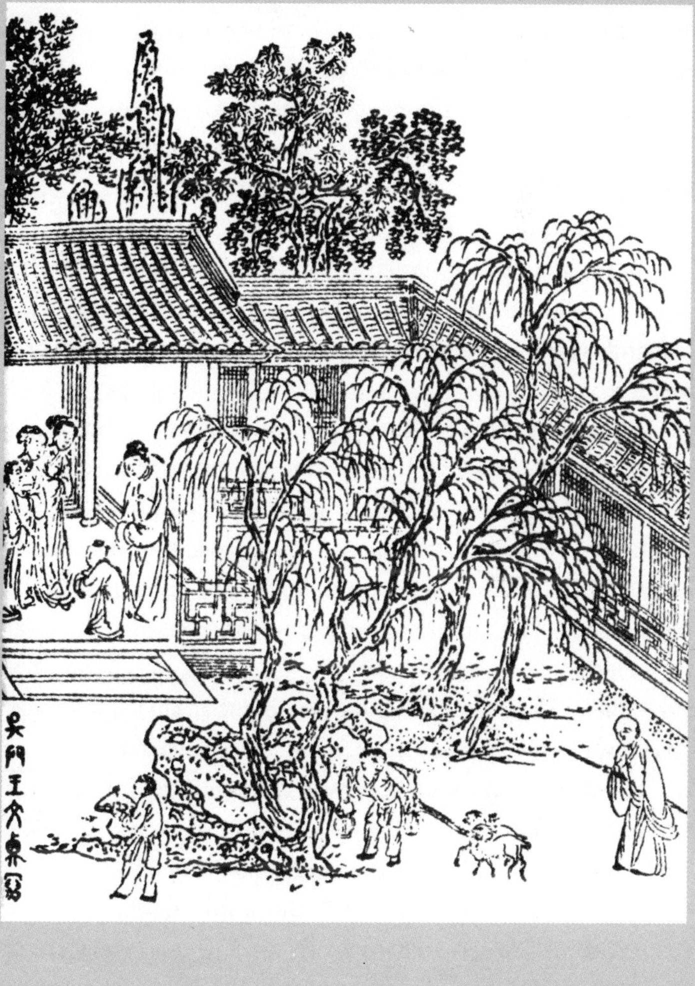
吳門王文衡寫

THE ROMANCE OF THE WESTERN CHAMBER

Sheng, the prefecture magistrate. I shall report these crimes to His Majesty and you will be punished according to the letter of the law."

With his lies being exposed, Zheng Heng got on his knees and begged for mercy.

"I'm so sorry! I lost my mind... I planned to trick Madame and Miss Cui so that I might wed the daughter before Zhang Sheng returned. I never thought I'd been exposed so quickly. Please general, have mercy on me. I'll cancel the wedding and Yingying shall be his."

It was only by this time that Madame Cui began to realize that it washer own nephew who had played a dirty trick. Regardless, he was still her nephew and General Du's threat unnerved her.

"Calm your wrath, General. He has admitted his fault and I implore you to allow him his freedom without any punishment" General Du turned to Zheng Heng and snapped, "If it were not for the good Madame's request, and that today is the honored day of my sworn brother's wedding, I would make sure you paid the price for your deception, you unscrupulous scoundrel! Now get out of here!"

Zheng Heng ignobly withdrew from the room in disgrace. On his way out of the temple he saw that Hongniang, Huan Lang, and the monks of the temple were all laughing at him. The shame was unbearable – how could a man of noble descent end up like this. He knew his life was already over, and upon exiting the temple he bumped his head to a tree and killed himself.

Madame Cui now realized the extent of her mistakes towards Zhang Sheng. She turned to him and said, "It's a rare honor for me to have both the general and the abbot to serve as the witness to this wedding. The feast is prepared – I suggest we begin."

All welcomed her suggestion. Hongniang threw her arms around Yingying in a happy embrace, and then accompanied her back to her quarters to get dressed for the wedding.

Zhang Sheng said to General Du, "If it were not for you, none of this could have happened. Twice you have saved me – I owe you my life!"

"Nonsense, don't mention it. You can always count on my help. My happiness at this day is exceeded only by your own – I wish you both many happy years together and undying love for each other."

Madame Cui invited General Du and the abbot to sit at the head of the table. Zhang Sheng and Yingying first bowed to Madame Cui, then to the abbot and General Du, and finally to each other. The assembled crowd then lavished them with wishes for longevity and happiness as they walked hand in hand into the bridal chamber.

The couple married happily thereafter, just like two lovebirds safe in their nest together.